pLACE
Of the
DAWN

The world is a better
and happier place in which
to live because of people
like Joan Earl

   Merry Christmas 1975
      from the author's brother.

   Bob Taylor

PLACE
OF THE
DAWN

GORDON
TAYLOR

HOLT, RINEHART AND WINSTON   NEW YORK

Published simultaneously in Canada by Holt, Rinehart
and Winston of Canada, Limited.

Library of Congress Cataloging in Publication Data
Taylor, Gordon, 1943–
Place of the dawn.
I. Title.
PZ4.T2357Pl   [PS3570.A9292]   813'.5'4   75–513
ISBN 0–03–014531–7

Grateful acknowledgment is made for use of eight
lines from "Two Songs from a Play" by William
Butler Yeats, from *Collected Poems of William Butler
Yeats,* copyright 1924 by The Macmillan Company,
renewed 1952 by Bertha Georgie Yeats. Reprinted by
permission of The Macmillan Company.

First Edition
Designer: Sandra Kandrac

Printed in the United States of America

FOR ROBERT AND ELIZABETH DARLEY-DORAN

Everything that man esteems
Endures a moment or a day.
Love's pleasure drives his love away,
The painter's brush consumes his dreams;
The herald's cry, the soldier's tread
Exhaust his glory and his might:
Whatever flames upon the night
Man's own resinous heart has fed.

—W. B. Yeats

MICHAEL
CROSSMAN

You probably haven't thought much about Anatolia lately, have you? Yes, I understand; don't apologize. But don't start smirking either, friend: I wasn't trying to denigrate you *or* the Turkish Republic, where I currently pay rent. I live in Turkey of my own free will, after all, so there must be something I like about it. I was merely stating what I take to be an interesting and somewhat puzzling fact, namely, that no one really pays much attention to what must be one of the world's most fascinating countries. Ask the average person what he knows about Turkey and except for the occasional mention of Turkish towels or shish kebab you will usually get a blank stare in return. I suppose it's partly because the Turks, an insular people, have never bothered to acquire the knack of cultivating a positive public image for themselves ("selling themselves," as we say in humanistic America). And so, Turkey has remained an acquired taste for some people and a virtual unknown quantity for most others.

I am one of those who have acquired the taste. Mind you, in Istanbul, that's not very difficult. I've been here for five years now, teaching English to the scions of the Turkish upper crust, and in that time I have become—shall we say—comfortable. Not "rooted," not "settled" really; just comfortable, glad to be here. Right now, sitting on my balcony in the early autumn sun, I can see the Russian merchant fleet carry on its incessant parade up and down the Bosporus. And tonight I will go alone or with friends to my favorite waterfront restaurant to drink and dream the night away. Yes, Istanbul is an easy taste to acquire. But I like the rest of the country, too. I like the peasants, with their contrariness and their basic decency. And the narrow river valleys where rows of poplars and vegetables crowd together under the rocky cliffs. I even like that barren mass they call the Anatolian plateau, in the spring with its vast carpet of green wheat and yellow flowers or in the shadows of a late summer afternoon when the eroded, golden hills seem almost to ache with weariness.

But, for me, as for any expatriate, there are times when the acquired taste goes bad, when I've asked myself, Why am I here with these people, with their impossible way of doing things, with their customs that defy all rational analysis? The feeling may be triggered by a stupid official, by a letter that doesn't arrive, by news of some unspeakable injustice, or by any one of a hundred minor annoyances that can occur in a given day. Or by something so overpowering and personal that I've felt lost, utterly without justification for being who I am or for living where I do.

I know it was like that this summer, for me and for Julia as well, when she came from America to "get away," to climb Hasan Gazi, and dig in ancient ruins; when she discovered far more than she expected at "the place of the dawn."

I'll start with Julia. Julia Warren, *née* Ross. I met her in college, where she was the female mainstay of the theater department. I was the stagehand who hung out in the wings, experiencing the tragedy of being her close friend instead of her lover. I was not alone in my worshipful attitude toward Julia. She easily provoked that kind of awe: the adulation that produces bushel baskets of poetry and buckets of self-hate. She had what is called "presence."

But Julia's intelligence, talent, and beauty made her not only an extraordinary human being, they made her a "prize catch." And she was caught by the end of her senior year. Joe Warren was the man who carried her off to suburbia. If there were ever a marriage made in heaven (or in Central Casting), it was that of Julia and Joe. I remember them appearing together in Albee's *The American Dream* at school: Joe, of course, playing the American Dream himself, with his close-clipped blond hair and quarterback's body straining the seams of a white sweater with the red and blue letter A, and Julia, supposedly playing a frumpy housewife, but looking just as beautiful as Joe. A year later, when we had graduated and I was dug into my earthen house on the plateau southeast of Ankara, their wedding picture came in the mail, accompanied by a letter from Julia saying how happy they both were. The photograph made them look like gods, like two people who had been specially chosen to breed for the future benefit of the human race. Every Christmas thereafter, during my two years with the Peace Corps, my two years with the army in Germany, and the last five years here in Istanbul, I got a card from Julia telling of Joe's rise in the New York financial world, of her own intermittent employment in advertising, and of their periodic hiking trips in the mountains of New England. And there would be another photograph with each card, the two of them looking even more impossibly Olympian as the years passed.

Then this year a letter arrived from Julia on the first of May bringing the news that *she* was planning a trip to Turkey in July and August. She was going to eastern Turkey under the auspices of something called American Expeditions Abroad, to work on the archaeological dig at Tanyeri. AEA, she explained, found people jobs with archaeological and scientific expeditions in return for contributions to those expeditions. I had long known about Tanyeri, though I had never made the trek to see it for myself. A remote Urartian site, it had received very little publicity compared to the more glamorous Greek and Roman excavations in the western part of Turkey. Tanyeri means literally "the place of the dawn," or the East in general; in Turkey it was virtually a byword for remoteness, a tiny village on the shores of a lake deep in the mountains south of Lake Van, in an area where the borders of Turkey, Iran, and Iraq run together and get lost among the rocks. Julia went on to tell how excited she was about the prospect of climbing Hasan Gazi, the volcano which overlooks Tanyeri and its lake, and she asked if it might be possible to stay with me when she came through Istanbul. The last paragraph informed me that Joe had been killed in a car crash in March, "while on his way to visit the family lawyer about our impending divorce." As in all the previous Christmas cards, there was no mention of children.

After reading the letter I did my very best to muster grief over Joe's death and sympathy for Julia, but in the end I could feel only a mixture of shock, surprise, and delight that a beautiful woman out of the past was coming to see me. I immediately went to the typewriter and banged out a letter saying yes, welcome, how nice to hear from you, sorry about everything that has gone wrong, I am here teaching, let me know when you're coming, and I'll meet you at the airport.

She did let me know, and exactly two months later, on Sunday afternoon, July 1, I took the bus out to Yeşilköy to welcome Julia to Turkey.

It was a filthy hot day along the Marmara, and it made the Istanbul airport that much harder to take. Torn apart and "undergoing renovation" since almost the dawn of time, Istanbul's Yesilköy Airfield appears to have been designed and built by a mixed bag of Greek and Armenian fanatics and donated to the Turkish government as the settlement of an old vendetta. It has all the problems of Istanbul without any of the attractions. Like the city itself, the airport consists of a ramshackle core surrounded by modern accretions, perpetually "under construction."

I made my way to the customs arrival hall amid the late afternoon heat, the honking, and the scream of turbines. As I walked into customs a supremely bored female voice announced in tortured English syllables the arrival of Flight 673, Turkish Airlines DC–10 service from Amsterdam, Julia's flight.

No doubt the jumbo jet was packed to the ceiling with Turkish workers returning to the old sod for a vacation. What an incredible flight that must have been: wall-to-wall moustaches; no inflight meals, just a bag of sunflower seeds for every passenger; enough cigarette smoke to clog a chimney.

I took a quick look around the arrival hall, which looks something like a warehouse where I used to work. I was standing at the eastern end with a small crowd that had gathered for the plane's arrival. To our left, against the south wall, a half-dozen customs inspectors and policemen lounged in front of the conveyor belt that brought in luggage from the cargo area. At the far end was Passport Control, and beyond that a bank of windows facing the sunlit runway. Nobody seemed particularly concerned about the horde that soon would descend upon us. The customs officials joked among themselves and gazed idly at the planes out on the runway. Two policemen were holding an impromptu boxing match. Another leaned against the wall and dragged on a cigarette. The mysterious East. I love it.

Several minutes later we saw the first of five buses disgorge its load of people outside the windows at the far end of the hall. Then another bus came, and another. Soon the hall had come alive with Turkish workers swarming into line at Passport Control, and the excited babble of their voices rose to a roar as they shouted and waved to relatives at my end of the room. I couldn't see Julia anywhere.

The growing crowd milled around in the center of the room, waiting for the baggage to arrive. Another bus pulled up outside the runway entrance to the hall, and I saw more passengers get out. These well-dressed people were undoubtedly part of Pan Am's Flight 618 from Rome, which had been announced over the PA a minute before. Another bus pulled in; more well-dressed tourists got out. Then another came. The first bus looked as if it were trying to move, but was blocked by one of the buses that had brought the Amsterdam passengers. The driver honked; the other driver honked back. It was getting hard to see the buses now, with all the people lined up outside the windows and those inside waiting for luggage. There were now about a hundred people milling around in the center of the hall. Over the PA the same bored woman announced something else, but above the din it was getting pretty hard to understand her.

Soon the customs hall had become a maelstrom of human beings, most of them darkly clad, animated Turks. The luggage had begun to arrive, but nobody seemed to be claiming any of it.

"Ahmet!" screamed an old man standing beside me.

8

"Baba!" a young man at the other end of the hall screamed in return, running the length of the customs hall into his father's eager embrace. The policeman stationed near the door to keep us out of the customs area separated them and sent the young man back to the ever-growing mass of people.

And I now saw why. The cases all had blue and white Pan American luggage tags on them, which meant that they belonged to those people still outside. I looked toward the luggage area and saw more cases than I ever knew existed piled in heaps upon the long, low rack in front of the conveyor belt. More and more continued to roll down the belt as a pair of moustachioed Sorcerer's Apprentices in threadbare khaki and off-white Rootie Kazootie caps tried frantically to cope with the flow. "*Kapat!*" they yelled, "Turn it off!" but nobody listened, unable to hear above the noise. Still no one from the seething mass in the center of the hall had claimed any of the mountain of luggage. A trickle of sweat ran down my nose and dropped off into space. I began to wonder if my deodorant would hold up.

Then, the milling crowd parted briefly, and I found myself looking at a tall blond woman wearing dark corduroy bell-bottoms, white tennis shoes, and a yellow blouse with the tails out. She had a red bandanna tied in her hair, a flight bag over her shoulder, and was carrying a mountaineer's ice axe. Julia. We both smiled and waved. She walked over to where I was standing, and I nervously managed to speak first.

"Hello! Welcome to the Pearl of the Orient."

"Thank you! Is it always like this?"

"Nearly. They've screwed up the bags, you know. The ones they've got now are for the Pan Am flight."

"I thought as much."

"Did you see the Pan Am plane?"

"Yes, a big jumbo jet."

"Oh, no!"

"Oh, yes!"

"What's that for?" I asked pointing to the ice axe.

"For the mountain I'm going to climb! Didn't I tell you?" She laughed.

The customs policeman came over at this point and asked Julia to go back to the main part of the hall. With a smile and a short wave, she disappeared again into the crowd.

By this time the people had begun to get impatient. The Amsterdam passengers, jammed together in the middle of the hall and barely clinging to sanity amid heat that had climbed into the nineties, began to generate small groups of two and three who shouted and cursed at the bewildered customs officials. The officials in turn yelled at the khaki-clad underlings, who yelled back at them amid wild gesticulation. From out on the runway a torrid late-afternoon sun sent its shafts of heat through the windows as buses continued to pull up in front of the arrival hall and unload passengers. Another announcement droned forth from the bored lady on the intercom. I didn't bother listening. The crowd continued to ebb and flow. Julia's blond head appeared briefly, engaged in conversation with a middle-aged fellow passenger. A tall, barrel-chested Turk with a fierce black moustache and the eyes of a dragon wandered around the perimeter of the crowd with a large stuffed falcon held in his left arm. Close by me on the right, the customs policeman leaned back in his chair and calmly smoked a cigarette, held *a la turca* between his thumb and index finger, the only person in the place who was enjoying himself.

Eventually the crisis resolved itself in the only way possible. The last of the Amsterdam passengers were stamped through Passport Control, and as the Pan Am passengers trickled into the hall and began claiming their luggage, the mountain of suitcases finally began to disappear. Eventually enough room was created so that the conveyor could start bringing in the luggage that should have been brought in first, and at last, over an hour after Julia had arrived, she pulled her baggage, a large lobster red backpack, off the conveyor belt.

She picked up her pack by the top of the frame and dragged it over to where I was standing. The customs policeman, still leaning back in the chair and now breathing through what must have been his tenth cigarette of the last hour, looked at us as though wakened from a trance. I looked down and asked him in Turkish if he wanted to look at the luggage. Moving in slow motion, the old man raised his head and eyebrows, meaning no, gestured toward the door with his left hand and, looking disdainfully away, brought the cigarette once more to his lips for the slowest, most sensual of drags. That was it. We walked out the door.

Outside the customs building a hot wind was still blowing in off the Marmara, and it dried some of the sweat off our bodies as we stopped briefly to breathe great smiling sighs of relief. The taxi drivers descended upon us in an instant. We took the nearest car, a mint-condition 1956 Chevy Belair with fender skirts, spinner hubcaps, and a string of blue evil-eye beads hanging from the rear-view mirror. Julia got in while a brief round of bargaining ensued between me and the driver, a short Sancho Panza type. I don't know why I bothered. The bargaining ended, as usual, in my total capitulation to the driver's exorbitant demands. So we got in and took off for Bebek. My week with Julia had begun.

We had a very full week, with lots of sightseeing and shopping and general tramping around. Julia loved Istanbul.

"It's like a wilderness," I remember her saying as we stood

on top of the Galata Tower and looked across the harbor to the domed, minaret-studded hills swarming with activity.

"Like a what?"

"I mean, it's not neat and organized, like most cities. It's more like a forest, with all the decaying things and the dead things and the living things tumbled together in a heap. And gorgeous."

About the middle of the week we went to a production of *Coriolanus* in Turkish at Rumeli Hisar, the gigantic castle on the Bosporus. We had a wonderful time, although we understood nothing. It was a very lavish production, with scores of extras and bright costumes and the illuminated stones of the castle walls rising all around us. At regular intervals another gigantic ship would materialize from behind one or another of the watchtowers, and the deep sound of its foghorn would echo across the dark waters. When Coriolanus returned to Rome in triumph from the war against the Volsci the cannons went off, skyrockets shot up, and hundreds of people suddenly appeared on the ramparts shouting and waving banners.

We talked and talked that week: about Julia's marriage, about my near-marriage the previous year, about the city and its people; and again we drew close, like the time in college, when Julia regarded me as her "best friend," the guy who was "like a brother" to her. And, as in college, by the end of the week she had become not so much a friend as a silver screen onto which I projected my most orgiastic fantasies. Had I not known better, I might even have called it love. I had been contented, you see, resigned to my lot and happy to be *hors de combat* after ending a long-term affair the preceding January. Then Julia appeared, and the neurotic longings of the newly thirty came gushing forth to engulf me. She was a reminder of all the things I hadn't done and would never do, the kind of vision that flashes by in the dark and leaves us aching at the sight.

Before I knew it Saturday had arrived. Julia was scheduled to leave on the train to Tatvan the next morning. We ate that night at Ruyam, the favorite waterfront restaurant of mine I mentioned earlier. The name means "my dream" in Turkish, and it's very appropriate, considering all the hours of inactivity I've spent there. I frequent Ruyam because the people know me, and because the furnishings are just shoddy enough to put me at ease. Salih Bey, the owner, sits at his raised desk in front of a large picture of Atatürk and glares down at the waiters scurrying about the room. In the middle of one wall hangs a massive, ornately framed mirror, which Salih Bey proudly claims was brought from "the seraglio." Out back is the open-air restaurant where I always sit in summer. Vines grow thickly on the trellis overhead, and no table will ever sit straight on the cobblestone courtyard. If you're in boring company you can always count on the foghorn of a passing ship to drown out conversation. Really an ideal sort of place.

Julia and I were greeted by Abdullah, who is my regular waiter and possibly the world's most obsequious human being. Abdullah is a sweet, thirty-ish little guy who wears a white coat almost as greasy as his hair and moustache, and whose face perpetually wears the tortured smile of a man drinking orange juice with chocolate cake. He welcomed us gleefully and bowed low—rubbing his palms together to get them well lubricated—then gestured with his right hand toward a corner table in the manner of a carnival magician unveiling his beautiful assistant.

As we sat down, Abdullah snatched a spotted cloth from under his arm and began snapping it around the table at invisible flecks of dust, then picked up our plates and used the cloth to polish them. That finished, he clasped his hands behind his back, bent expectantly at the waist, and with a dazzling smile exposed his teeth for our inspection.

By this time both Julia and I were fighting desperately to control an incipient fit of the giggles. I managed to summon some Turkish.

"Ne var, Abdullah?"

"Her şey var, Monsieur."

"What do you have, Abdullah?" was answered by, "We have everything, Monsieur." The reply was an exaggeration no stupider than my question. I've been eating at Ruyam for five years, and I ought to know what they have. We decided on some mixed hors d'oeuvres and swordfish kebab.

We had a moment's peace before the food was served. I looked across the table at Julia and feasted my eyes for an instant before following her gaze out onto the water. In the middle of the black strait a tanker the size of the Empire State Building was sliding by to the north, its decks a blaze of light. A moment of aching silence passed, then a tremendous WOOOOooooonk rolled across the water and off the hills as several thousand tons of steel and crude oil prepared to make the turn by Rumeli Hisari.

Suddenly the hors d'oeuvres arrived: lots of plates with bits of this and slices of that and blobs of other things. Abdullah grandiloquently presented us with half a dozen dishes while one of his young slaves yanked the cork out of a tall, cold bottle of white wine.

We sat and ate under the vines by the water's edge. A light breeze was blowing from the south, lifting and playing with the flimsy napkins in our laps. Back of us, on the road that winds north along the shore, the traffic set up its low, elemental murmur beneath our voices as we spoke.

"What are you thinking about?" I asked, as she gazed across the water.

"The train tomorrow. Tanyeri. And the mountain. What is it like out there?"

"It's very empty, very poor, and very mountainous. There are lots of Kurds where you're going."

"What are Kurds?"

"The people who live in that area, and over the border in Iran and Iraq. They speak Kurdish, which is close to Persian."

"So they don't speak any Turkish then?"

"Yes, all the men speak Turkish, because they all have to serve in the Turkish army. But the women speak only Kurdish. They've been there a long time, you know—mentioned in writings as far back as Sumerian times. Xenophon and the Ten Thousand had to fight their way past the Kurds in order to get to the Black Sea."

"I won't ask who Xenophon and the Ten Thousand were."

"Xenophon and the Ten Thousand were an intrepid band of creative, freedom-loving, democratic Greeks who signed on as mercenaries to a Persian prince, got trapped in Mesopotamia and made their way back to Greece by plundering the countryside and killing anyone who got in their way."

"Hmm. They sound like a nasty bunch."

"Yes, they all had blond hair and blue eyes, and they voted Republican. When they got back to Byzantium they celebrated by founding the world's first Rotary Club."

"Really." Julia smiled as she took a stab at a stuffed pepper. "Did they go through Tanyeri, these Ten Thousand?"

"Probably not, actually. They probably passed a bit west of there, around the west end of Lake Van."

"Have you talked to anyone who has actually been there?" she asked.

"Yes, I know several people who've been out there. They all raved about it, but hated the roads. They are *bombok*."

"Which means . . . ?"

"For shit." She laughed. "Nobody goes there, you see. There is the citadel, and I guess one or two villages around the lake—which is not very big—and the mountain. Nothing."

"Or everything," she said, "if you like mountains, which I do."

"Have you had much experience at climbing?" I remembered how impressed I had been with her pack and ice axe on the day she arrived.

"A little. When I was younger I had some training at summer camp. Joe and I used to go in the Adirondacks and up in New Hampshire a lot. No heavy stuff, though: you know, driving pitons into sheer cliff faces and all that. If I can't walk up it I want no part of it. I'm in this for the view."

"They say Hasan Gazi is easy."

"Yes, a walk-up, really, with the last three or four thousand feet on snow. I brought some four-point instep crampons, which I hope will be enough."

"I don't know anything about it," I said. "My God, you look excited—like a kid on Christmas Eve."

"Yes," she said, smiling broadly and looking directly at me, "this is something I've been looking forward to for three months. I don't think I've ever felt more excited than I do now. This is a fascinating place. I feel a bit strange sometimes about getting here the way I did—inheriting all that money after Joe's death and the rest of it. But I can't help it if I feel wonderful and free of it all at last."

"When I read your letter in May I was really shocked. I guess I'm really very old-fashioned about things like that. I wondered if *anything* is possible between two people these days. Two people like you who had been together for so long. And now you mention the climbing you did together . . ."

"Yes," she said with a sad sort of smile, "that was supposed to keep the marriage viable. Common interests, you know. But it wasn't Joe I disliked, it was the institution. And Joe's success only made it worse."

"You don't really mean Joe loved success more than he loved you."

"No," she answered slowly, fighting for the words, "I know it sounds awful and clichéd, but everything seemed to go right for us, and it drove me crazy. I mean the better things got, the higher Joe rose, the more I felt constricted."

"Constricted? How?"

"Constricted by the things I wasn't doing. I mean, it's almost as if people like me—you know, people who went to college and vote Left—it's as if we have a built-in discontent that just never goes away. Like with Joe and me. He had his thing, which was economic planning. Systems analysis. 'The real world,' he said. And I respected that. I envied him, really. But in the end it never satisfied *me*, no matter how much I loved him. And the part-time jobs never satisfied me, either, no matter how enjoyable they were. They were always things I did because of him or because of us, not because of me. That sounds very selfish, I know, but I always ended up feeling that it was the institution of marriage, not Julia herself, that was defining my life. And even though it made me feel stupid, the discontent just kept on growing. Eventually it started coming out, against my will, all over the place."

"Like what, for example?"

"Fights, quarrels about petty things mostly. The things themselves didn't matter much. It was the discontent with myself that did it."

"You really loved each other then?" I asked.

"Oh, of course, Mike. And honestly, we had many wonderful times together. That's why my depressions made me feel so stupid. By all objective standards there was no reason for them to exist. Joe was very kind and handsome and interesting. But I couldn't take it, and one day last March, out of the blue, I just told him I wanted out."

"And did he say much?"

"Yes, he was heartbroken, but he got used to the idea soon enough. I hadn't been making life very pleasant for him anyway. But he got killed and ironically I got everything." Another wistful, disillusioned smile crossed her aristocratic face. "Poor guy," she said. "I should never have married anybody in the first place."

I stared off over the water, trying desperately to think of something wise and comforting to tell her. I couldn't think of a thing.

"What do you think, Mike?" she asked, now looking straight at me. "Do you think I was right?" I looked at her a second, then back at the water and north to the lighted battlements of Rumeli Hisari.

"I—I don't know, Julia," I stammered. "Honestly, I can't think of anything to say."

Mercifully, Abdullah picked this moment to show up with our swordfish. He set down the kebabs and began whisking away the hors d'oeuvre plates. About fifty yards down the road a taxi driver leaned on his horn, which came to life in a blaring, off-key rendition of *"La Cucaracha."* Julia stopped chewing her food, her eyes wide with astonishment. The horn repeated its honking sounds. We looked at each other and dissolved in laughter. I noticed several other people doing the same. It's impossible to take anything seriously when someone is playing *"La Cucaracha"* on the auto horn.

The rest of the evening passed quietly, with me dreaming of love and Julia dreaming of her mountain in the east. More ships passed, the breeze stirred the vine leaves overhead, and we floated on toward Sunday in a narcotic trance. We finished eating and paid the bill. I left Abdullah a gigantic tip—you know, twenty-five cents, something like that. He responded with enough bows to fracture his spinal column, while Julia flashed him a dazzling smile. We swept out through Ruyam's front room, past Salih Bey at his post, and started walking back to my place.

Fifteen minutes later we walked into the darkness of my living room. And here of course I would like to say that we fell into each other's arms for a final night of unbridled lust and romantic love. But . . . beautiful women have never yet melted at my approach, and I don't think they ever will. Julia didn't. There was no reason why she should have.

We talked for a few minutes on the balcony, mostly about getting to the train the next morning and when she would be coming back from Tanyeri. Then she went off to bed, and I stayed there in the dark to smoke my first cigarette in many months. Above me the faint laughter of neighbors' voices floated out and mingled with the distant whish of traffic on the road below. Tall cypresses, black spears of foliage almost close enough to touch, framed my view of the lights of Asia winking across the strait. That old romantic masochism flowed through me with its delicious ache, and I could feel myself suspended in space, drifting, a lonely, tragic figure who soon would have to get up and go to the john. Visions of Julia and every other woman I'd been close to swarmed in my head: dreams, shimmering bubbles that burst when I touched them. But a voice said, *She's not a dream, stupid: she's a person. She doesn't exist to satisfy your longings for love and fulfillment. She doesn't define her life in terms of you.* And in answer there was no voice at all.

On Sunday morning, July 8, Julia and I crossed the strait to Haydarpasha, where she left on the Lake Van Express.

MARY
SCHULLER

It all began innocuously enough. I met Julia Warren when she got off the train at Tatvan on Monday afternoon, July 9. It was my job to meet her (I'm the "liaison" at Tanyeri for American Expeditions Abroad, which means that I meet their people and look after them in addition to my regular chores), but I was happy to do it and very anxious to see another American woman. For four weeks I had been the only woman at the Tanyeri site, and although I suppose I should be used to the isolation after three summers in this country, it's always nice to have someone else around.

I got into Tatvan early—around noon—with the expedition minibus and Turgut, the driver. We had about another hour before the train came in, so I went to get some lunch and told Turgut I'd meet him later up on the platform. From where I got out of the van I could look north to the landing and see the big white ship that carries boxcars and passengers to Van at the east end of the lake. Beyond that, to the northeast, the white cone of Süphan Dagh floated above the haze.

I was back again, hot and dirty, on the streets of Tatvan, but it felt good to be there.

After a leisurely meal at my usual restaurant across from the Atatürk statue I started wandering toward the station through the dusty back streets of the town. They were swarming with children playing football, running, fighting, and yelling at me: "TourEEst! TourEEst!" and then the inevitable *"Alman? Alman?"* to ask if I am German. As usual I did my best to be friendly and relaxed, but it's never easy.

As I approached the station I saw a small group of children pointing to the mountains and shouting *"Tren geldi! Tren geldi!"*—"The train is coming!" I saw a long plume of black smoke and beneath it a thin gray chain of coaches moving across the mass of Nemrut Dagh. They were right. For once the train was on time.

I thought of the tired people on board and remembered my first ride into Tatvan on the Van express three summers before, when I had been a junior in college, off on my first major dig, with no experience of Turkey at all. I especially remember awakening one morning on that train in the upper valley of the Murat.

I had shared the compartment all the way from Istanbul with five other people: a husband and wife, and the man's three brothers. I sat by the door. The two seats on my left were occupied by two of the brothers. The third brother sat opposite me, the wife next to him, and the husband by the window.

He was a short but handsome man, of that unyouthful, indeterminate age Turks assume after having done their military service, acquired a wife, and grown a moustache. He looked thirty-five; he was probably twenty-five. But his dark, handsome face radiated the ferocious intensity of a man clinging to a cliff edge with his fingernails.

24

If you could have seen his arms, you would understand part of his desperation. The skin from the tips of his unmoving fingers to his elbows was horribly burned and blistered. Beneath a thick coating of greasy salve that glistened in the sunlight, blotches of yellow pus stood out against the reddened flesh. His wife, a young woman with a sad brown face, sat in silence beside him, resting her head on his shoulder, mopping his brow with wet cloths and occasionally doling out orange capsules from a plastic bottle. All day long and into the night, as the train traversed the heart of Anatolia, he sat motionless by the window, his unbandaged arms raised off his lap, his hands covered only by a pathetic stained handkerchief to keep off the dust and the flies. Except for an occasional sigh of pain, he never said a word.

At that time I knew very little Turkish, but gradually, through the broken English of one brother and interpretations by other passengers who came in to offer sympathy, I found out what had happened. The man and his wife had been living in Istanbul when fire had destroyed their house only three days before, killing their two children. The young father had burned his arms trying to save the children, one a boy three years old and the other a baby of six months. The brothers had gone to Istanbul to bring the couple back to their village.

The eldest brother passed around a copy of one of the more sensational Istanbul dailies, a paper whose name in English means "Good Morning." There on the front page, right alongside the picture of a seminude belly dancer with stars on her nipples, were photos of the man and woman who sat opposite me. It was a very big spread. The bigger of two pictures showed the young man, obviously in shock, standing outside the smoldering building and holding his burned arms in front of him. His wife and another man supported him on either side. The other photograph showed only the wife, standing alone slightly bent over, her face contorted in unspeakable horror.

I wanted to cry when I saw that picture, but I looked over at the couple and choked back my tears. Seeing them there across from me, the wife leaning on her husband's shoulder, their faces blank and sated with grief, I knew that any weeping of mine would be mere self-indulgence. And what could anyone do? Say I'm sorry? Give them food? They had food, and the burned man couldn't eat anyway. Give them money? For what? For doctors? There were no doctors where they were going. They were leaving the best doctors behind them, and anyway it would take more than an ordinary G.P. to heal those burns. It seemed certain the man would lose his arms if something wasn't done, but who out here could do anything? Even today, I'm sure he must have lost them.

But somehow he held on as the aching minutes gathered into hours and the train rolled across the steppe. I tried to read, tried walking up and down in the corridor, but I found my whole body focused on him there at the window, focused on suffering that went beyond anything I had known. He was awesome.

About sunrise of the second day he finally broke. We had made up the compartment into *couchettes* for the night, and lying on my top bunk, I was awakened by sounds higher pitched and more insistent than the steady roar and clack of the rails. "Allahallah . . . allahallah," someone was sobbing. I looked over the edge of my bunk and saw them huddled together below me, the wife covering her husband's face with caresses, the brothers weeping with bowed heads as the young man vented his grief into the pillow. Outside over a range of mountains the rising sun threw yellow glints and spangles of glare on the dirty window glass of our compartment. Fifty feet below the railbed, clicking past in a blur, the Murat

26

poured its green, frothing water through a narrow gorge. This time I couldn't help it, and I turned to the wall and cried.

I spent the rest of that morning in the dining car watching the river and wishing there were less pain in the world. Long ago I had seen Disney movies of animals—American bison, wildebeests, I can't remember which—animals moving in a herd, gathering in mute, helpless sympathy around one of their number who was sick and dying. It seemed somewhat that way with these people, as if they were responding to an instinct deeper and more elemental than that which told them to seek a doctor, an instinct which said, *Go home; band together; close the circle around yourselves.* I could not say that they were wrong.

By midmorning we had climbed out of the Murat Valley onto the Plain of Muş, green and dotted white with storks. We waited there for half an hour while an ancient Norwegian steam locomotive was coupled on to help the diesel over the next range. From there the track rose again into high, barren mountains. At one stopping place high on the mountain wall water gushed out of the rocks to our left in a long, white cascade and flowed under the railbed on its way to the round valley spread beneath us on the right. The conductors, knowing the stations well, jumped off as soon as the train stopped and filled their canteens at the waterfall. At first a few passengers followed suit; then seemingly half the train climbed down and ran toward the gushing water with every conceivable type of container. Soon the whistle shrieked, and there was a mad, laughing dash back to the coaches as the train lurched forward on the last leg to Tatvan.

By then it was near noon, and we were only an hour or so from the lake. I wandered toward the front of the train and found my compartment empty. The four brothers and the woman had gone, and no one had taken their places. Where had they gone? I asked a man in the next compartment. They had gotten off two or three hours before, back on the other side of Muş. Back in the gorge, no doubt, at one of those stops with a few trees, a cluster of huts beside the river, and barren mountains unfolding into nowhere. *He'll die there,* I thought, *he'll die there.* What strange, beautiful people they were.

Before long we were crossing a plateau at an altitude of over eight thousand feet. Long concrete tunnels covered the tracks to keep the snow off in winter. When we passed through them black smoke from the engine was swept back into the cars and filled our nostrils with hot, rancid dust. That was the ultimate discomfort, though, for soon we came through the last gap in the mountains and saw far below us the gray houses of Tatvan, and beyond them the great lake itself, blue and sparkling and rimmed with snowy mountains. I've made the trip three times now, but there was never an arrival like that first one. I felt as though my whole future was bound up in the sight of that town and that lake. And of course it was: my involvement with Tanyeri, my love for Kemal, and the emotions that will keep me coming back for a long time. Despite everything that has happened, I love it here.

It takes about fifteen minutes for the train to arrive at Tatvan after first being sighted on the mountainside, those fifteen minutes being taken up by the long series of snaking loops necessary to bring the track down from its great height. I waited on the platform with about thirty other people. The hawkers were everywhere, selling water, soda pop, sandwiches, candy, shirts, and even shoelaces. One little boy around ten years old appeared silently in front of me, a tray full of hard candies hung around his neck. I told him I had just eaten and didn't want any. He didn't seem to hear, didn't say anything, just stood there. I told him again I didn't want any, but still he gaped at me. At that moment a black phantom loomed into view on my right. It was a woman (at least I had to presume it was a woman), old, judging by her voice, completely swathed in a black *çarşaf*, and coming toward me with her right hand extended. (Her left hand was being used to keep the veil closed tightly around her.) Though initially a bit put out at the idea of giving money to someone I couldn't even see, on an impulse I dug into my jeans and handed the woman a lira. She gave me a perfunctory thank you and scurried off to her burrow. The young candy seller, still staring up at me, threw up his hands and gave me a look a wounded disgust, as if to say, "You can give money to that old beggar but can't give anything to a hard-working boy like me." Sigh. He was right, of course. Once again I started digging into my pocket. When the Van express finally pulled in at 1:15 I had a pocketful of hard candies.

I didn't have much trouble recognizing Julia when she stepped down from the sleeping car. She had told me by letter to expect a blond woman with a red backpack, and I'm sure there was no one else remotely close to that description in a radius of five hundred miles. I walked over to where she was standing and introduced myself.

"Hello, you must be Julia."

"Yes, and you're Mary?"

"That's right. How was your trip?"

"Wonderful!" She made quite an impression standing there, not only because of her movie-star looks but because of the way she carried the pack: absolutely straight, as if it were floating on her shoulders. The platform was full of people: passengers, relatives, hawkers, children, and the inevitable handful of hippies bound for Afghanistan and dope with a capital D. And how they all stared! Julia might as well have been from outer space.

"Have you eaten yet?" I asked.

"Yes, on the train."

"Good, then we can get going right away. If I can locate the driver." I looked around the crowd for Turgut but couldn't see him anywhere.

"They really like to look, don't they?" Julia said.

"You've noticed? It's just something you have to get used to. Of course, if you're like me you never will." We looked over at a small group of peasants some ten yards away who appeared by their expressions to be witnessing an H-bomb blast. I spied the tall form of Turgut on the edge of the crowd, and he signaled to me.

"Come on," I said, "we can talk while we're bouncing along the road."

"Yes, I've heard about this road. *Bombok,* is that the word?"

I laughed. "Yes, that's the word, but respectable ladies like us don't use it in public."

"Do respectable ladies carry packs on their backs?"

"Yes, but usually they're filled with firewood or cow dung."

Turgut led us to the minibus, a blue Ford van that was new when I started at Tanyeri but which now seems afflicted with every known automotive disease. Everybody knew that we needed a new vehicle, but Kemal declared that it had to last at least one more season. Ours is not one of the more well-funded expeditions, which is why AEA contributors like Julia are so welcome.

Julia and I climbed into the back along with her pack, which had some sort of pickaxe strapped to it. I asked what it was.

"That's an ice axe for mountain climbing," I was informed. "I've been planning on going up Hasan Gazi since I read the blurb in the AEA brochure."

Turgut cranked up the engine and we shot off through the town.

"Have you done much climbing in the past?" I asked. I was impressed, I must confess. I'm not very athletic.

"A little. Enough to know that I enjoy it. I've heard Hasan Gazi is just a walk-up anyway."

"That's what they say. It doesn't really look very steep, but I've never known anyone who's gone up."

"Really? Hasn't anyone in past years done it?"

"No. Only some Swiss tourists who came in last summer and spent three days at it. Remember, we haven't really had very many AEA participants come to Tanyeri so far. And no one on the staff has been equipped for it. Naturally, none of the villagers would dream of wasting their time on such a thing." The air inside the van lay thick with heat, while outside, the dusty streets of Tatvan swarmed with peasants, animals, children, and occasional women in their obscene black veils. Hard to imagine any of them climbing a fourteen thousand-foot mountain. "Why?" they would say with looks of total incomprehension. Julia was talking.

". . . Hope I can find someone to go along, because it's always best to have friends. Not only for company, but because it's safer."

"I think we can arrange something. Sinan has often talked about going, but no one else has ever been available or willing."

"Who is—"

"Oh, I'm sorry. Sinan is one of the other staff. He's a graduate student, like me."

"How many people do you have at Tanyeri right now?"

"Right now only five full-time people. We're a very small expedition, really. Frankly, that's why we appreciate contributors like you. We only have you and one other man now —a man from Michigan named Frank Martin—but we have about a dozen people slated as guests in August."

"Are we the only English-speaking people then?"

"No, no. Kemal speaks English perfectly: he's my professor in Cincinnati. Sinan speaks very good English also. He was an exchange student in the States several years ago."

I turned to look out the window and felt a tremendous crash jolt the chassis of the minibus. That was the sound of the vehicle's undercarriage receiving its first taste of grim reality as we drove off the last stretch of asphalt in Tatvan and set forth on the boulder-strewn waste leading to Tanyeri. Seventy kilometers of axle-crunching madness lay ahead, with two mountains and a final eight thousand-foot pass to climb. And it would take about four hours to get through all of it.

"This is it!" I proclaimed above the din. "Grin and bear it."

There is something about a road like the one to Tanyeri that totally destroys my desire to talk. I think Julia felt the same way. We kept on for a while, talking about Tanyeri, the work, the summer finds, and the people there now, but soon the conversation died out and the road took over, rattling our bones, feeding us its dust and jolts. Julia seemed to bear up pretty well, all things considered. Junior League, that's what she kept reminding me of. Like the women at the rummage sales where we used to scrounge clothing in college. Elegance in blue jeans. What is she doing here?

An unfair question really: What were any of us doing there? And having asked the question, this is as good a time as any to provide part of the answer, at least the part that deals with Tanyeri itself, what it is and what we hope to find there. The best way, I suppose, would be to quote the section on Tanyeri that appears in the brochure put out by American Expeditions Abroad, the "blurb" that Julia referred to earlier, and which I wrote.

(Expedition No. 5) Archaeology in Eastern Anatolia. (a) July 1–29; (b) July 30–Aug. 26

Dr. Kemal Altay of the Cincinnati Archaeological Institute returns to Turkey for his fourth season of excavations at the Tanyeri citadel, south of Lake Van in southeastern Anatolia. Tanyeri was a major outpost of Urartu, or the Kingdom of Van, which flourished in this area from the ninth to the sixth centuries B.C. The citadel served as an important defensive outpost against Assyrian encroachment. Later, after the fall of Urartu c. 600 B.C., it is thought to have been used by local tribes as a base for raids against the Armenians, who were infiltrating the country from the west.

The primary activity of this season's campaign will be excavation of the newly discovered temple to Haldi, chief god of the Urartian pantheon. It is hoped that the temple will provide important new clues to the understanding of Urartian religion. Evidence from previous campaigns indicated that the Tanyeri citadel was destroyed by fire around 700 B.C. Additional finds from that holocaust are also expected to be uncovered.

The Tanyeri site itself, though quite remote, is one of the most impressive in the Middle East, being situated on a promontory overlooking Lake Tanyeri at the base of 13,989-foot Hasan Gazi Dagh. Hasan Gazi, a dormant volcano whose last recorded eruption occurred in 1753, is named for a Seljuk Turkish warrior who died in a skirmish with Byzantine forces near Tanyeri in 1071. His remains are buried in a tomb on the mountain's northeast slope.

Forty-five minutes after leaving Tatvan we were grinding uphill in first gear on our way over the first of the mountains we had to cross. Appallingly close on the right—and then on the left as we switched back—the road's edge dropped away almost vertically to a broad valley bisected by a small river and dotted with nomads' black tents. Across the valley, back in the direction of Tatvan, a long mountain ridge lay shadowed by a white stratum of clouds that hovered along the crest.

Turgut had a time of it, fighting to maintain momentum on the narrow road as he constantly swerved to avoid rocks and chuckholes. Most of the time it wasn't worth the effort, since he only hit others. To the right of the shift lever sat a large plastic jerry can whose brown water Turgut occasionally poured over the straining gearbox. The water glugged out in brown sloshes on the gearbox housing and trickled back along the dusty floorboards to where we sat. It probably did about as much good as those blue beads dangling from the rear-view mirror, or the sign on the dash that piously announced, "What Allah says, will be." Cast your fate to the wind, in other words. Good advice for anyone traveling by road in this country.

We gained the summit and started slowly down the switchbacks on the other side. Below us stretched more hills and another green, empty valley and beyond that more and more mountains, gray and jagged, dappled white with snow and the shadows cast by a hundred clouds skimming over their summits and trailing mist down the sides. Off to the southeast I could see the nameless ten thousand-foot range that formed the last barrier between us and Tanyeri. That was about twenty miles away—over an hour on this road.

"Are you beginning to feel sorry that you came?" I shouted to Julia above the crash and whine of metal.

She laughed and shook her head. "As long as I don't die I'll be all right."

"Don't worry, Turgut is really a very careful driver."

"Oh, I'm not worried about that! I'm afraid one of these times the van will just fall apart and roll over a cliff!" She wasn't the only one.

"In another hour and a half we'll be at the top of the pass above Tanyeri. When you see that you'll know it's worth it."

She looked at me when I said that, and I could see the excitement ignite in her eyes. I must have been the same way three years before.

We reached the summit of Kavak Pass at 4:30. Turgut parked the minibus while Julia and I stood on a nearby outcrop and gaped. Hasan Gazi had come into view only minutes before as we labored up the last thousand feet to the top of the pass. Like many skyscrapers, surrounded by giants, it can only be seen by those who are relatively close. And we were very close: less than ten miles away. Hasan Gazi lay directly before us to the southeast, a gigantic cone with snow glistening on the summit and cascading in long, white ribbons down the sides. A solitary tuft of cloud floated along the east side near the snow line. The silence was broken only by the clicking contractions of the minibus as its engine cooled.

"Gorgeous, isn't it?" I whispered, feeling very much like a little girl revealing a secret hideaway to a friend.

"Wonderful," Julia answered. "And intimidating."

Yes, indeed. Almost fourteen thousand feet of intimidation, to be exact. Not terribly steep, but high—and massive. A long walk to the summit. At the base of Hasan Gazi, completely enfolded by its bulk, Tanyeri lake lay blue and placid, a tiny puddle collecting water from the melting snows. I pointed out the castle in the middle of the south shore and to the right of it Tanyeri village itself, a cluster of tiny shapes built slightly above the narrow alluvial plain. Three kilometers farther along the shore, we could just make out the houses of Gaziova, the tiny Kurdish village at the other end of the lake.

But Hasan Gazi dominated everything. *Try not to look at it. Try.* Julia wasn't trying. Neither was Turgut, a man who had lived within sight of the mountain for virtually all of his thirty-five years. He had rolled a cigarette and now sat on his haunches breathing its smoke into the wind, his eyes fixed, like ours, on the mountain.

Julia spoke softly, an ironical smile at the corners of her mouth.

"Shangri-la. It's like Shangri-la."

Yes, I had to admit it looked like that. And as I've said before I really do love it there. But for a moment I was tempted to open my mouth and tell her all the reasons why it wasn't Shangri-la: about blood feuds and serfdom, and poverty hard as stone. But I didn't say anything. She would find out soon enough, and from the way she had said it she probably knew already. Julia had certainly seen other villages in Turkey. These just happened to be a bit more remote and situated in a far more beautiful setting.

We climbed back in the van and rode down into the valley. A few minutes later we passed a young shepherd, who waved at us as his sheep obliviously munched their way across the mountainside. From where he stood, green, rounded slopes covered with yellow and white flowers fell off on all sides. More switchbacks. And more. And, again, ruts and boulders as we tortuously wound down the road into the Tanyeri Valley. Twenty minutes later the road had leveled off, and after stopping several times to ford irrigation ditches that had been diverted through the road, we drove the last few kilometers into the village.

We entered the village square, a dusty, open area dominated by a large plane tree. Turgut pulled up in front of the *çayhane*—the village teahouse—where he had several cases of tea and sugar to deliver. Julia and I got out to stretch our legs. Towering above us the mountain seemed almost close enough to touch. The usual group of men sat in their gray eminence on the shady side of the *çayhane*. We had seen their wives and daughters hoeing the fields as we drove in. They sat and stared at us. One of the older ones I recognized as a man who had labored for us the two previous summers. Smiling deferentially, he stood and bowed to me. Mostly they were looking at the new arrival with the golden hair.

When Turgut came out of the teahouse we left Tanyeri, heading east. Once past the rows of poplars at the town's edge we could see the castle below us, half a mile away, perched on its rock by the lake. A short distance farther along we turned off on the narrow track that cuts across the fields to the castle. More of Tanyeri's females were out hoeing in their baggy trousers and white *çarşafs*. They stopped and waved happily as we bounced by.

By this time it was well past five o'clock, and I expected to see some of the workers from the dig walking down the road. The majority of them usually leave around five o'clock, though they occasionally stay later. I saw no one on the path, however, and I presumed that Kemal was keeping them overtime for something special.

I was wrong. As our weary van heaved its aching axles the last few feet up the side of the castle rock and took a hard left through the gates, I saw where all the workers were. They were gathered in a mass near the big headquarters tent, making a considerable noise. A few of them turned around as we stopped, but most remained absorbed in the commotion in front of Kemal's tent.

I got out, and Julia followed. I could hear several voices shouting, among them Kemal's.

"My God," she said, "what's happening?"

"I don't know. Whatever it is, it's certainly unusual." I couldn't see anything except the backs of thirty peasants, all wearing flat caps and gray trousers patched beyond belief. The sun still blazed in the heavens, but in typical fashion they all had their long-sleeved shirts buttoned to the throat and their jackets draped cloaklike across their shoulders.

I walked around to the left, trying to get a better view of the action. Julia followed, looking nonchalant about the whole thing. It didn't look as if there would be much of a welcome for her, but I didn't know what to do about it. No sense taking her away and pretending this didn't exist. Whatever *this* was. I still didn't know.

Kemal saw me as I reached the edge of the crowd and gave me one of his heaven-help-us looks, eyes turned skyward for an instant. No wonder. It was quite a scene. The entire archaeological team (except for me) was lined up in front of the headquarters tent: Kemal and Bekir Bey, the co-leaders, and their assistants, Mahmut and Sinan. To the left of Kemal stood his foreman, a Tanyeri villager named Orhan, who has been with him since the beginning. Behind them, inside the tent, were three of the villagers who work with us on pottery restoration, and at the entrance I could see the black, bespectacled face of Frank Martin, our other AEA contributor.

Sinan was talking now, angrily and very fast, so fast that I couldn't begin to understand him. He was facing a large man in a navy blue jacket and black riding boots that came up to the knee. This man was Hasso, one of the more prominent of the small group of workers who came from Gaziova, the Kurdish village at the eastern end of the lake. He was a man whose massive size and heavy, moustachioed features would have naturally drawn attention in a crowd. He dwarfed Sinan, who was by no means small or plain himself. Hasso's fellow workers, perhaps ten in number, stood behind him. They were all Kurds (though no stranger could have discerned this), and I guessed that must have had something to do with the argument that was raging.

Kemal seemed to have had his say and was standing with his hands shoved into his blue jeans, looking very worried. In the few seconds after I had arrived the argument seemed to have taken a turn for the worse. Sinan and Hasso had inched close to each other at this point, and the Kurds from Gaziova looked sullen and nervous as waves of muttering resentment coursed through the crowd of Tanyeri Turks standing around and behind them.

What happened next passed so quickly that I could scarcely assimilate it. I was watching Kemal, who at the time appeared to be on the verge of breaking into the argument. Suddenly his head jerked up and he looked straight at Sinan in disbelief. Sinan had just uttered a word which I had no trouble at all in understanding. The word was *eşek*. It means "ass," and it is not the kind of word that anyone should use in Turkey unless he has a gun or a very extensive insurance policy.

Hasso now demonstrated why. There was a quick movement, a wrench in Hasso's body, and a knife suddenly appeared in his right hand, glinting silver in the sunlight before it streaked in a wide, rushing arc toward Sinan's body. Sinan jumped back, but part of Hasso's body hid my view and I couldn't see if the knife had struck its target. Then as the knife came up again to strike, a white-shirted blur materialized, moving swiftly from left to right, and attached itself to Hasso's body. It was Orhan, the foreman. Clubbing Hasso in the back of the neck with his left hand, Orhan knocked him off balance. Then with a swiftness and strength the like of which I have never seen, he grabbed Hasso through the crotch and around the right arm and simply flung him some six feet to the left. There was no finesse, no grace, to the motion. It happened with the suddenness and brute force that I have seen peasants use to pick up struggling sheep and dump them on the ground for shearing. The knife went flying, and Hasso fell in the dust as the crowd let out a collective gasp of astonishment. The whole incident, from Sinan's insult to Hasso's fall in the dust, had taken about ten seconds.

Hasso sprang to his feet and began shouting insults at everyone. By now, however, several of his compatriots from Gaziova had run over to restrain him, and the violence seemed to have peaked. Kemal's voice once again made itself heard. He shouted to restrain the Turks, who seemed ready *en masse* to finish off the job that Orhan had begun. Then, turning to Hasso, he rushed through several convoluted and to me incomprehensible sentences ending with a very clear command to get out now.

Hasso did so. It was clear that if he didn't there would be a riot, with the Kurds very much on the losing side. With a final curse at the assembled company, Hasso strode fiercely toward a large black horse tethered by the gate, mounted, and rode off. The other Kurds followed on foot.

Kemal shouted at the remaining crowd of Tanyeri workers urging them to break up and go home. They began to drift off, talking excitedly among themselves. Kemal had turned to Sinan, who seemed to have been grazed slightly by the knife.

"What was that all about?" Julia asked. "Did you understand it?" I'd forgotten she was even there. No more than three minutes had passed since we had gotten out of the van.

"I don't know. They were talking so fast I couldn't make out much. I'm sorry this had to happen. Really, we've never had anything like this before."

"Don't worry, Mary. It was fantastic, really. Where else could I have seen something like that?"

"Well, I can think of quite a few places in the States," I said, trying to laugh. After the shock of the fight, seeing Sinan almost stabbed by that wild man, and now realizing that this paying guest from America had arrived at our camp in the middle of a brawl and near-riot, I felt stunned.

I decided against introducing her to Kemal. He was deep in agitated conversation with Bekir Bey and Sinan. Several of the workers, including Orhan, and Frank Martin stood around listening. Sinan seemed to be getting the worst of it, no doubt on account of his hotheaded insult to Hasso. They all turned and went into the headquarters tent. It looked like the makings of a fine mess. What was behind it? I wondered.

"I'm sorry about this," I said turning to Julia. "Normally I would introduce you to Kemal and the others. But obviously they're busy right now. Let's go to our tent and you can get settled."

Turgut got her pack from the minibus, and we walked over to the east side of the citadel, past the storage and restoration tents, the mess tent, the latrine, and finally to the last row of eight conical tents where our merry crew hangs out in the summer.

Only five of the tents were occupied at the time: one each for Kemal, Bekir Bey, Mahmut, and me, and one that Frank and Sinan were sharing. The remaining three we held in reserve for occasional visitors and for the other expedition contributors from AEA whom we expected in August. I took Julia to my tent and showed her where she would be living for the next three weeks. Luckily the bed had been made up as I had ordered, so at least that part of her welcome was right.

By then it was about 5:30, and after leaving Julia alone to unpack and relax, I walked to the headquarters tent hoping to see Kemal and find out the cause of all the commotion. Coming around the mess tent, I nearly collided with Sinan, who was walking along with his head bowed, like a man on his way to the gallows.

"Sinan!"

"Hello, Mary." A sheepish smile creased his brown face, lifting his moustache slightly.

"Sinan, what was all that about? Are you hurt?"

"No, the knife only touched me." He pulled aside his shirt

and displayed a bandaged area about two inches long just to the right of his navel. It seemed absurdly trivial considering the near-riot that had produced it.

"But what happened, Sinan? Why were you arguing?"

"It was nothing. I should not have gotten so angry." He added, bitterly, "But these people—they are always complaining—about nothing!"

He looked away, and I could see it was not the time to be interrogating him about anything.

"Cheer up, Sinan. I'll go talk to Kemal. I was on my way there anyway."

"I will see you later," he said and walked away toward his tent.

I had taken two steps when Frank Martin's large form swung into view. He was wearing his usual checked shirt and open smile. Frank was the man the workers called the "Arab," because he was black. This amused Frank, and because I liked him I didn't tell him that, for these people, "Arab" was a term of contempt, the functional equivalent of "nigger." Frank had come all the way from Jackson, Michigan, to help out with our dig. He was forty-eight, a widower, a parole officer, and an ex-teacher. He mentioned once that he had a son, but never talked about him further. Frank was friendly and open and kind, and often I found myself looking at him with that helpless feeling I get in crowded public places when I see a particularly vulnerable face and think, My God, I hope he isn't lonely.

"Hi, Mary," he greeted me, "how was your trip?"

"Bumpy as usual."

"Tatvan just as beautiful as ever?" He made it rhyme with batman.

"Yes," I said, and laughed. "Frank, what was all the argument about anyway? Sinan didn't tell me a thing.'

"Yeah, he's probably feeling pretty low. Kemal really gave him hell. Of course I didn't understand a word they said, and I don't know what caused the fight or anything. I was just following Sinan, hoping he would tell me."

"Well, I'll go talk to Kemal and find out what happened. I guess you can go and console Sinan."

"Yeah," he paused and slowly shook his head, "that boy almost got his guts ripped out."

I walked through the last row of tents and out into the open parade area, where only a few minutes before the fight had taken place. Straight ahead, the sun hovered over the western wall of the fortress, bathing my face in its warmth, now welcome against the encroaching coolness of night. The workers had gone. Only a few men remained talking near the south gate. Behind them Hasan Gazi rose immense and white, the clouds now scoured from the summit.

Bekir Bey, our expedition co-leader, came out of the headquarters tent just as I arrived. He smiled politely and nodded his head in greeting. Bekir Bey is a slight, balding man who wears dark-rimmed glasses and looks very much like the professor he is. Because we don't talk much to each other, I still use the formal *Bey* with his name. This is partly because his English is as tentative as my Turkish and partly because I sleep with his colleague, an arrangement he undoubtedly frowns upon. But Bekir Bey doesn't talk much to anyone. He is a totally dedicated archaeologist, a very private man who is quite content to pursue his studies and nothing else. He and Mahmut, his protégé, are the monks of the Tanyeri expedition. They socialize very little with any of us and spend most of their time sifting shards or reading under the gas lamp until all hours of the night. He and I only nod at each other and smile.

Kemal was alone inside at the table, puffing furiously on

his pipe amid the usual chaos of books and papers. He rose smiling when he saw me and pulled the pipe out of his teeth long enough for me to lean over for a kiss. I'm not going to set forth a detailed description of my lover, except to note that he is short, dark, and handsome. Five inches shorter than my five feet ten, to be exact. I do a lot of leaning over for kisses.

"Did our new arrival get settled all right?" he asked, sitting back down in his canvas chair. I walked around behind Kemal and sat in the empty chair beside him.

"Yes, she's unpacking now. I'll have to go back and check on her though. She probably wants to take a shower." Which would require some instructions about valves and things. "We certainly picked a terrible time to drive in."

This was Kemal's cue to tell me what had brought about the incredible scene out in front, but it looked for a moment as if he intended to say nothing. For a few seconds his expression stayed hidden behind the pipestem and a cloud of smoke. Then as the smoke dissipated I could see the sadness etched on his face.

"I don't know, Mary," he said slowly. "You want me to explain what happened, but I really cannot do it. I can tell you the events, but why the events produced the end result, why Sinan was nearly cut open, I do not know."

He paused. A hoarse voice sounded in the background, coming from the general direction of the mess tent. Ali preparing dinner for 6:30. Kemal went on.

"It started around five o'clock, when the men were leaving for home. They tell me that for some reason one Turk from Tanyeri and one Kurd from Gaziova started to argue. We don't know why, they just did. Soon the two groups were shouting at each other, calling each other thieves and giaours and everything else. So we all came out and tried to stop it.

44

Then this Hasso, who is one of their leaders, breaks in and turns on me. He tells me to stay out of it. He says I am always on the side of the Tanyeri people, the 'pig-eating Shias' he calls them. He asks why I don't hire more Gaziova men—they have many men with no work in their village. Well, I tried to break in, but he was screaming like a wild man. That was about the time I saw you. Then Sinan broke in and started shouting back at him, and in a few seconds we almost had a murder. It is all so stupid."

Kemal stopped talking and went back to his pipe, drawing out the smoke in long, disconsolate drags. He took it personally when his people "went wrong." A year before he had begun the process of becoming an American citizen, but I knew that he had only done it in the knowledge that as an archaeologist he would be able to return to Turkey every summer. He still cared very much about these people, and incidents like this fight hurt him deeply.

And as he said, it really was very stupid. Anyone with sense knew that the Kurd's accusations were unjust. Kemal had consistently dealt fairly with both villages, whose religious and ethnic differences meant nothing to him. We would certainly have hired more men from Gaziova, but there simply was no money for it in this year's budget. But of course no one believed this, neither the Kurds nor the Turks. It was incredible to them that any American expedition could ever be short of money. But Kemal Bey, the men would say, doesn't your government give money for this? What about all those astronauts gathering rocks on the moon? They weren't so dumb, these peasants.

"Are the Kurds going to stay?" I asked. That was all we needed now, a boycott.

"Yes, they'll stay. They need the money. Tomorrow it will be forgotten." We pay what everybody else pays diggers in

Turkey, thirty Turkish lira a day, or a little over two dollars. Still, Kemal was right: they needed the money and they would stay.

"At least that savage Hasso is gone," I said. He was not the kind of person I ever wanted to see again.

"Yes," said Kemal and turned to me. Then in a somewhat lighter tone he said, "You know, Mary, as an American you should be more respectful toward 'that savage,' as you call him. I found out some very interesting things about this man Hasso from Bekir just before you came."

"Like what?"

"Well, he was a great war hero, that's what."

"Really? Which war?"

"The Korean War. He fought with the Turkish Army in Korea. Bekir told me he killed many Chinese. He got a medal from the American army."

"Well . . ." What else was I going to say? It seemed a bit incongruous, still and all. In my mind I couldn't imagine that hard, bearlike man, with his black boots and moustache, in the uniform of an ordinary soldier, slogging along the 38th Parallel, or holding back the Chinese Army from a trench. My Korean War had been fought on late-night television, with William Holden bombing the bridges at Toko-ri while Grace Kelly waited for him in Japan, and Mickey Rooney lay dying in a ditch with a green scarf around his neck. I didn't associate it with Kurdish peasants on horseback.

"Even if he was a hero, I'm still glad he's gone," I said.

Kemal laughed gently. "How was the trip to Tatvan?" he asked.

"The usual. Turgut got the wine. Two cases of it. Somehow the van made it back, though Turgut spent half the time pouring water on the gearbox."

"That crazy fool," Kemal laughed. "Why does he do that anyway?" And he went on laughing.

46

"I thought you could tell me. You're the man, the one who's supposed to know about mechanical things."

Kemal was still laughing. "All I know," he said, "is that it doesn't make much sense to pour water on a gearbox cover. But who knows? Maybe he's right. Maybe it will help the bus to make it through the summer. I don't know what we'll do if it doesn't."

"Anything new out of the temple?"

"No, pretty much the same things." By that he meant pieces of broken pottery, charred bits of wood, and an arrowhead or two. So far the excavation of the Haldi temple had produced relatively little.

"Oh, by the way," said Kemal, reaching out across the pile of papers on the table, "you got a letter." He handed me a pretty blue aerogram with familiar writing on it. It was from my mother in New Jersey. I glanced at the table in front of us and spied amid the piles of paper an opened envelope whose contents had been read and reinserted. The writing on it was also familiar, that of Kemal's wife.

"How is Ayla?" I asked, trying to sound casual, yet as sincere as possible. It was the kind of conventional, meaningless inquiry I've often resolved to avoid, but it came out anyway.

"She is fine."

I almost said, "And the children?" but caught myself. I might have gone on, "And your in-laws? And your parents, who arranged the marriage for you in the first place?" Kemal did not need such badgering, but I was often tempted to break out of my "understanding, patient" role and strike at the people whose archaic customs forced me to share the affections of this human being with a woman who did not love him, a woman who had simply been sold to the family for use in perpetuating their line. And inevitably the qualities that made him so lovable—the kindness, the decency, the unwillingness to disrupt the lives of so many people—kept him from making the kind of clean break that was necessary if we were to escape from the present impasse. But what would that mean to Kemal? Ayla would certainly win possession of the children, and would, just as certainly, go back to Istanbul to live with her parents. This, Kemal did not want, for he loved his two daughters very much and wanted them to grow up with him in the States. Then there was the matter of his career, which would very possibly be jeopardized by any move to divorce his wife and marry me, his "young American assistant." Kemal's field was Urartian archaeology; he had to work in Turkey. And in Turkey the granting of permits to dig was an uncertain business at best, a business that Kemal's present father-in-law, a former cabinet minister, could easily make very difficult for him if he decided vengeance was in order. All things considered, it was a fine mess.

We sat in silence for some seconds as I read my mother's letter. It was mostly about visits to relatives and other events of the outside world. The light within the tent dimmed as the afternoon passed into evening. I got up to go.

"I'd better see if Julia needs help."

"Yes, do that," Kemal said and rose with love in his eyes. We kissed again and this time held each other for a moment, Kemal's head resting on my chest, my fingers running through his black, curly hair. There are times when I like being five inches taller than Kemal, and this is one of them. For a few seconds it doesn't matter that he is married to another woman and that this woman is more beautiful than I. She can't rest her chin on his head the way I can, and she never will.

Ali the cook brought forth his usual menu that night: pilaf, eggplant kebab, and lots of tomatoes. It makes a great meal, but I was at the point where I never wanted to see another eggplant or tomato again. "They're in season," Ali would say, and I would suppress the urge to grab one of those fat, shiny aubergines and hit him with it. Only the wine, which we had three times a week, made the monotony bearable.

There were ten of us at the table: the five regular staff people (Kemal, Bekir Bey, Sinan, Mahmut, and I), Frank and Julia, our two guest participants, and at the far end, talking among themselves, Orhan and the two guards who went on duty at sundown. I introduced Julia to everyone, and they seemed duly impressed. She had showered and looked even more elegant than before.

We were all a bit embarrassed after the afternoon's violence. Kemal started off by apologizing for the incident and wishing that Julia's stay would be more pleasant than her arrival. Then Sinan apologized for his outburst.

"Please, don't apologize," Julia said to Sinan. "It was very exciting. Besides, it's not your fault that someone tried to kill you."

"Yes," Sinan answered, "but I had made him do it."

"Sinan means that he called him a name," I said, "and that provoked the attack."

"I was foolish," said Sinan somewhat sullenly. He lowered his head and dug into the plate of pilaf.

"Do you think there will be any more danger from the man who attacked you?" Julia asked.

"We don't think so," Kemal answered. "As long as Sinan does not go over to the village looking for trouble it will surely be forgotten."

"Why don't we change the subject and talk about the work in progress," I suggested.

"Yes," said Julia, "I think Sinan would enjoy that more." He looked up from his plate and gave her an embarrassed smile. He was a very handsome boy when he wasn't frowning.

"Have you found anything at the temple yet?" Julia asked, turning to Kemal.

"Nothing much," he said as he grabbed a hunk of bread from the basket. "We've been somewhat disappointed so far. We're finding out more about it, but still we haven't had the big breakthrough we're looking for."

"What sort of breakthrough is that?"

"Well, I can't say exactly. Something—we don't know what—that will give us some solid insights into Urartian religion. We've identified seventy-nine gods of Urartu—the chief god being Haldi—but we would like more information on how they were worshiped, their origins, that sort of thing.

"You know, originally we were hoping that our digs here would prove that the Tanyeri fortress and surrounding area were actually Musasir, which was the holy city of Urartu, dedicated to Haldi. At first it looked like a possibility. The first trench we dug, in the summer of 1967, showed that Tanyeri was only inhabited from approximately 800 to 600 B.C. Most importantly, though, we found massive evidence of destruction by fire around 700 B.C.—approximately 725 to 700."

"How do you know this?" Julia asked.

"By carbon dating, mostly. We send samples of the charred wood to Chicago for analysis. Anyway, we know from the chronicles of the Assyrians that the city of Musasir was destroyed by the Assyrian king, Sargon II, and his armies in 714 B.C. There was a relief found at a place called Khorsabad, south of here, in Iraq, that shows the sack of the city and the destruction of the temple."

"So the Tanyeri castle was destroyed about the same time?"

"Exactly. And we know that Musasir has to be in this general area somewhere, though most archaeologists think it was a bit farther east of here. If Tanyeri had turned out to be Musasir, it would have been a major find and would certainly have given us a lot of information on Urartian religion."

"What happened to change your mind?" Julia asked.

"Well, first of all, I was never sure, because the Assyrians were not the only people who attacked Urartu at that time. In 714 Urartu was attacked by the Assyrians from the south and the Scythians from the north. So we know that it could have been them instead of the Assyrians."

"Who were the Scythians?"

"They were nomads, Aryan invaders from Central Asia. They attacked Urartu many times. Eventually they spread west, along with other nomads, and brought about the collapse of Phrygia."

"Phrygia?" Frank now broke in. "You mean Gordium."

"Yes," said Kemal, "but don't let me get started on the situation there."

"I still don't understand how you're so certain that Tanyeri is not the holy city," said Julia.

"Well, it just became obvious that it wasn't. In the first place, at the level where Tanyeri was destroyed by fire we found many arrowheads that we could identify as Scythian. They're a very definite type, quite different from the usual Urartian arrowheads, which are flat and broad, shaped rather like leaves. The Scythian arrowheads are longer and narrower, with three blades. And very often on the socket they have a small hook. I'll show them to you later, if you like."

"Of course," said Julia, "I would like to see them. So this means that Tanyeri was destroyed by the Scythians and not the Assyrians?"

"Yes, and the final blow to our theory came last summer when we were digging in front of the palace. We found a stone with an inscription that tells us very clearly that Tanyeri is not Musasir. Its name was Halaini."

"So that was a big disappointment."

"Yes, but we have found many fine things, and there is much left to do. We still hope to find more, especially at the temple. You have probably read about the *karasy* we found last summer in the wine cellars."

"No, I don't remember."

"Ah, then you must see them. Enormous storage jars for tribute goods. We'll show them to you later."

"Kemal," Frank interjected in his low, rolling voice, "I've often wondered why you still keep all these things here. I would have thought you would send them off to the museum by now. For safekeeping, if nothing else."

"Really, Frank," I answered, "they're a lot safer here than on that road to Tatvan. Besides, we want them here so the village can have a museum. With some restoration done on the castle, and a small museum—and of course a new road in here from Tatvan—they might get some tourists out here."

Julia flinched. "Tourists? That sounds ominous."

"Yes, I know it does," I answered, "but I don't think there will ever be enough tourists to change things drastically. It's just too remote. Think of these people, though, living in mud houses, buried under ten feet of snow in winter, threshing their wheat with wooden sledges in the summer. A little money would help them a lot. From the top of Kavak Pass this place looks like Shangri-la, but I think you can see it isn't. There is no work besides farming here and not much of that. Both villages have men off working in Germany and dozens more that have applied to go. The ones who stay behind just scrape along with nothing but pride to fall back on. In a situation like that the slightest thing, like this afternoon, is enough to set them off."

Sinan now spoke for the first time. "Really, Mary, we must be honest about this. You make it sound as if they only fight because they are proud and frustrated. But why are they frustrated? Because they have no land! The peasants do not own this land, after all. Two big families own most of the land in Tanyeri, and all of Gaziova belongs to only one man. He lives in Ankara."

"One man owns the whole village?" Frank asked incredulously.

"Yes, he is a member of Parliament. He owns several villages in this province."

"My God . . ." Julia said.

Our voices fell silent, leaving behind the clatter of dishes and the sounds of people eating. Like discussing the weather on a rainy day there was a futility in the very mention of these people and their poverty that made it an automatic conversational dead end. But as always the image of the villagers hovered in the back of my mind overshadowing my life, like the mountain that looked down upon us all. Nobody starved in this valley. Nobody froze to death in winter. Total catastrophe never quite arrived, except when the earth moved and brought their mud houses down upon them. But nobody seemed to be advancing either. The peasants huddled together beneath the mountain and clung desperately to the past, to a way of life that had enabled them to survive in a land desiccated and ravaged by the three thousand-year occupation of their own species. The deer had gone centuries ago, and the lions soon after. Wolves were rumored to exist. A handful of bears still roamed in Hakkâri. Trees clung to the bare mountainsides in scattered patches, but the vast, ancient forests were not even a memory. Yet the people survived, hard and enduring like the rocks that jutted skeletally from the eroded hillsides. They had killed many things in their struggle to endure. And they still had not prevailed.

Later that night Julia and Frank came with Kemal and me to the expedition "museum," a long wooden shed that serves as a temporary home for the artifacts we've unearthed so far.

We were looking at the twelve giant storage jars that we had found in the citadel's wine cellars the previous summer.

"They're immense," said Julia. We had only a kerosene lantern with us, but it was enough to illuminate the two ghostly rows of *karasy*, six on a side, that formed an aisle down the middle of the storage shed. She was right; they are immense, approximately six feet high by five feet in girth, each with cuneiform markings denoting its capacity.

"We are fairly certain that they were used to store goods that had been taxed," Kemal said. "They would then have been part of the annual tribute required by the king."

"And how do you know this?" Julia asked.

"We've inferred it from the slab that Kemal mentioned at dinner," I said. "Come on, it's at the other end." We walked down the rows of jars, with Kemal holding the lantern and leading the way. The stela was in a dark corner resting against the wall, a stone slab some four feet by three feet, covered with neat cuneiform characters.

"What does it say? Can you read it?" Julia asked me.

"Of course," I said. "I wouldn't be worth much if I couldn't."

"What language is it in? Urartian?"

"Yes, but the alphabet is Assyrian cuneiform. It says, 'I, Ishpuini, son of Sarduri, servant of the god Haldi, faithful pastor of the nation, with the aid of Haldi and the force of troops, captured the city of Halaini and enslaved its King Urzana. I spared his life on condition that he pay tribute. This is the tribute required of Halaini: forty-one minas of pure gold, thirty-seven minas of silver, ten thousand minas of copper.' It goes on naming tribute items: cattle, horses, grain . . . everything you can think of."

"Is there anything more?" she asked.

"Yes, after describing the tribute it says, 'I, Ishpuini, son of Sarduri, servant of Haldi, do not fear opposition. I am ruler of Biaini'—that means Urartu—'and the conqueror of hostile nations, the lord of Tushpa and the Sea of Nairi. Whosoever destroys this writing, whoever breaks this tablet, whoever commits such a crime, may the gods Haldi, Teisheba, and Shivini destroy his name and grind his lineage to dust.' That's the end."

"Very well read," said Kemal. "I would give you an 'A' for that."

"Thank you, professor." It goes without saying that I had practically memorized it.

"What were those last two places you read?" Frank asked.

"Let's see. Tushpa—that's their capital city, now Van. And the Sea of Nairi is Lake Van."

"Tushpa. I wouldn't mind being king of that myself," Frank mused.

"Really, Frank," Julia said with a dubious smile. Frank laughed.

After another ten minutes in the shed looking at our collection, Kemal suggested that we walk into the village for some tea at the *çayhane*. I went to get Sinan, who had been in his tent reading, and the five of us (minus Bekir Bey and Mahmut who, as usual, cheerfully declined an invitation to come along) walked out of the south gate and down the path that led to Tanyeri.

The light of the waning moon filtered down, illuminating the dusty ruts that cut across the fields to the main road. Perched on the hillside, slightly above the precious level land that was reserved for crops, the village itself lay in virtual darkness broken only by the scattered glint of candles and kerosene lamps. Above that the mountain slumbered in its pale blanket of snow.

We go often to the *çayhane* at night. Nothing ever happens there except conversation, and often there is very little of that. We sit and drink our tea at a table in the open air, lighted only by the stars and the faint glow of a lantern hanging on the side of the building. We face south, directly toward the summit of Hasan Gazi. Before us the village square is dominated by a large plane tree whose black, leafy form stands just to the right of the mountain's white summit. There are several other tables scattered about. Most are populated with dark knots of peasants who lean together and talk in low mutters. From inside the teahouse comes the muffled clamor of voices punctuated by the clack of backgammon pieces and dice, the sound of maleness, of men so thoroughly dominant in their own society that they don't know what to do with themselves. A cat wanders across the square; a peasant comes by leading a donkey loaded with straw. Nothing happens. Nothing. We talk, drink our tea, and sit as the mountain lays its glory and its thrall over our lives. Enchantment stiffens into boredom. Life once again becomes impossibly long. And a few minutes later we return across the fields to the castle and the lake and the ineffably beautiful landscape that says, *I am lost in time. I will never go away.*

That Monday night we arrived at the *çayhane* around nine o'clock. Kemal went in to order tea while we found a table outside and managed to round up five battered chairs. The tea arrived, five tiny tulip-shaped glasses with two rock-hard lumps of sugar on every saucer. Julia dropped in her sugar and began looking for something to stir it with. I asked the man for spoons; he always forgets.

"I just reminded him to bring some spoons," I told Julia, "in this part of Turkey you rarely get a spoon with your tea."

"How do they expect you to stir in the sugar?"

"They don't. You're supposed to hold the sugar in your mouth and drink through it. Like this."

I demonstrated. Noticing this, a grizzled old man drinking his tea at the next table (a man who like the rest had been watching us intently) got our attention by opening his own mouth for our inspection and displaying the lump of sugar and a scattering of rotten teeth. "Ah, yes," we said, "very good," and thanked him profusely for the demonstration. He turned back to his partners at the table and had a good laugh at the crazy foreigners who didn't even know how to drink tea.

"Julia," Kemal said, "Mary tells me that you are interested in climbing Hasan Gazi."

"I'm not just interested; I'm planning on it. I've got the equipment, and I'm going to do it." She was facing me in the darkness, with only a corona of yellow light from the lantern surrounding her head.

"We had some Swiss tourists come in here last year to climb it."

"That's what Mary told me. How long did it take them?"

"I don't remember really. Do you, Sinan?"

"Yes, it was about two days I think. I think these Swiss people were real experts, though. They said it was very boring. Over four thousand meters, and it's boring! So I think they like going straight up, with ropes and things like that. On Hasan Gazi you just walk. They said there was only one interesting part and that was a cliff that runs along the very top. You can see it in the day."

"Yes, I've seen it," Julia said. "What's the best way up?"

"The best way up is on the east side. I have looked at the maps and talked to the people here and they say that east is the best way."

"So you've thought of going up yourself."

"Yes, many times," Sinan said, "but I have not had the time and the equipment. And, of course, nobody to go with. All these lazy cowards I work with . . ." he said, gesturing toward Kemal and me.

"I won't deny it," I said, "not the lazy part anyway."

"I have an excellent excuse," said Kemal. "I'm in charge of this expedition. I can't take off three days."

"Frank?" Julia asked.

Frank looked startled for a second, then laughed. "Me? I never thought of it. It looks a little high for an old man like me to be trying on foot. Anyway, where would I get equipment?"

"I think we can find something," said Kemal. "We may be able to borrow some things from the local army gendarmes. Let me ask."

Julia spoke to Sinan again. "I'm interested in hearing more about what the Swiss said. This cliff you say runs along the top, do you have to climb it to reach the summit?"

"No, no. Listen. You cannot go straight up from here because there is a big rockslide area on this side. Big, big rocks that fell from the top. Very difficult to pass. Then at the top you have this cliff running along, like a wall, or—what do you call it on a castle?"

"Rampart?" I volunteered.

"That's it—rampart. Like a rampart. But it's only along the top on this side. To get around it, you go straight up the middle from here, then go left to the northeast side, then go up that way. The Swiss people said it's easy. You just walk."

"Oh, is that all?" asked Frank. "That's good, just walk up fourteen thousand feet. Hell, my feet get sore even thinking about it."

"But Frank," said Sinan, "those people said the view is wonderful. You can see Hakkâri in the southeast, Süphan in the north, and Ararat in the northeast. It must be fantastic."

"Marvelous," said Julia. "But why is it necessary to go up the east side? Wouldn't it be just as easy, and maybe a little shorter, to go up the west?"

"Well, maybe a little shorter, but not much," said Sinan. "And it is the east side that is more interesting. On the west there is better grass; you have many sheep. On the east there are many big rocks, so there are no sheep."

"And no people."

"Yes. Also on the east there is the tomb of Hasan Gazi."

"Oh yes, the tomb! I had forgotten about it. Where is it? What is it like?"

"Well I don't know what it's like because I've never been there. But according to the maps it is about halfway down the northeastern slope of the mountain. There is a small hole— ah, depression I think you say—that the volcano made."

"You mean like a crater."

"Yes, it's a crater, that's the word. Quite small, though. The tomb is in there."

"But you've never seen it, Sinan?"

"No."

"I have," said Kemal through the bit of the pipe he was now lighting.

"When did you go?" I asked. He had never told me of going up there.

"I went five years ago," he said, "during one of the preliminary survey trips we made to Tanyeri. Bekir and I went up one day. Only as far as the tomb. That was far enough, really. It took us the better part of a day just to get up there, and it was after dark when we got back."

"What is it like?" Julia asked.

"Like nothing," said Kemal, drawing on his pipe. "There is only the remains of a small building, with a heap of stones inside and an old grave marker."

"It sounds very disappointing," Julia said.

"It's not, though. It is not disappointing at all. At least, it wasn't for me. When we arrived, there must have been twenty-five peasants up there—men, women, and children. They were from Tanyeri, and they were celebrating a religious holiday. You see, the people here are called Alevi. They are Shia Muslims, which means they are not orthodox. It's very difficult to explain, but basically it means they have slightly different practices, especially when it comes to holy days. This day I visited the tomb was one of them. They were observing the martyrdom of one of their saints."

"Martyred by whom?" Julia asked.

"By the Sunni—the orthodox factions—usually."

"What were they fighting about?"

"They were fighting for power, of course. Basically the Shia think that one man—Ali, the son-in-law of Mohammed—should have been caliph instead of the man who killed him. Don't ask me too much about these things, because I don't know very much. They really don't interest me."

"I didn't mean to sidetrack you," Julia said. "I'm mostly interested in hearing about the tomb."

Kemal sat next to me in the darkness puffing on his pipe. I could barely make out his features as he spoke. "Well, as I said, when Bekir and I arrived, there was a group of peasants, and they had just made *kurban*—they had sacrificed a young cow, a heifer, I should say. There was a flat white rock in front of the tomb, I remember, and it had been hollowed out to make a bowl. It was about one meter high and maybe the same in diameter. They must have held the heifer's throat over the rock when they cut it, because the bowl in the rock was full of blood. I remember the dark streaks on the side of the stone where the blood had overflowed. There was blood everywhere, on the ground and in spots on the foreheads of all the children, who ran around laughing and playing. The peasants had butchered the cow, and the carcass was lying there, off to one side. Several of their dogs were chewing on the bones. They were cooking the meat when we arrived. We got there just in time for a feast, actually."

"It sounds fantastic," said Julia.

"Really it was. For me, as an archaeologist, it was like stepping back several thousand years in time. I don't mean that it is an unusual occurrence. Animal sacrifice is normal in

Turkey. We have it all the time. We will have it in—what, two weeks? when the Kurban Bayram comes. But seeing it up there on that mountainside, beside that tomb, with nothing around but those ancient stones, it was something different."

"So it was the sacrifice, not the tomb, that was impressive," I said.

"Not entirely. The tomb was impressive in its own way. It was so *desolate*, you see. There was no roof, and the walls had crumbled away. Inside we could see only a heap of rock over the grave—no sarcophagus, nothing—and against the back wall a slab with Arabic script on it."

"What did it say?" Julia asked, her eyes riveted on Kemal.

"I don't remember exactly; I didn't want to stay and look. In the middle of the left wall I remember there was a small ... niche. In this niche a candle was burning. And this is the part I remember most vividly of all. I walked into the tomb ahead of Bekir. Outside the children were playing, and the blood was drying on the stones. Above us we could see the summit of the mountain. It was ... just nothing. I looked at the pile of rocks, then at the gravestone. My eyes rested briefly on the script, but I didn't try to make it out. Then I turned to the left, and saw the candle for the first time. Just as I noticed the candle a shadow fell across the tomb and the flame blew out. I tell you, I was stunned. Bekir and I looked at each other, and the look I saw in his eyes almost frightened me out of my wits. We walked out of the tomb—the rubble, I should say—and I decided I'd had enough of Hasan Gazi for one day."

"Wow," Julia breathed, "so did you come down right away?"

"No," Kemal laughed, "I think we both wanted to, but of course the peasants insisted that we should stay to eat with them. And of course we did. It is never wise to refuse the hospitality of Turkish peasants, and after that incident in the tomb we were especially anxious to please Allah." He laughed at the memory, hesitating before he spoke. "Then, when we were finished eating, Bekir and I, the two intellectual professors from Istanbul, actually agreed to do the *namaz* with these peasants."

"What!"

Sinan and I said it at the same time.

"Yes," said Kemal, "we actually turned to the south, got down on some grass mats, and did the prayers."

I could hardly speak. I just couldn't believe it. "Kemal," I said, "that's amazing! You! You really must have been frightened!"

He smiled and sucked on his pipe. "Yes," he said, chuckling, "I guess I was. It's very funny now, but then it just seemed like the only thing to do.

"But Sinan," Kemal continued, pointing at him with the stem of his pipe, "you must absolutely promise never to tell Bekir—or Mahmut—what I just said. He would die of embarrassment if anyone knew. And I would lose a friend."

"Don't worry," Sinan responded with a smile.

"Kemal, I really want to thank you for telling that story," Frank declared. "After hearing about that blood bowl and the shadow and thinking about my sore feet, now I *know* I don't want to go."

That got a laugh all around. We sat and drank our tea in the darkness while Kemal continued puffing on his pipe.

"I didn't want to discourage you with that story, Frank," he said. "I think you should go. The tomb is very interesting and beautiful in its way. But," he added quietly, "it is quite desolate. It is nothing, really."

At that moment a man appeared in the dim light, emerging from the darkness under the plane tree. He carried a *saz* —a Turkish lute—with a tassel dangling from its long, slender neck. I had never seen him before in the village, but he looked like a typical peasant with his nondescript clothing and his deeply lined, brown face. Several of the men seated about greeted the newcomer, and he returned their greetings. He was an *aşik*, a minstrel.

The man sat down by the corner of the *çayhane*, where the lantern illuminated the right side of his face. He placed his cap upside down on a nearby table, as an invitation to anyone who wished to contribute. The faint yellow glow made him look old beyond reckoning. His gray hair was sparse, and age had limned a deep pattern of shadow in his flesh.

The minstrel struck a chord, twanged one particular string several times for tuning, then began to play, the chords rolling forth from the *saz* in jangling, rhythmic blocks of sound. The music swelled, then fell to a murmur as the man's voice lifted into the darkness.

It was a song I had heard several times before, a ballad about endless wandering and lost love:

> *I see my love on the mountain,*
> *In the folds of a shadow high*
> *Where the flowers are carpets of gold,*
> *I see and wander on.*

The voice poured out and filled the night with quavering, tremulous sounds that to western ears hardly seemed to be melody at all. But they *were* melody, and they were *right*, like the feel of a Strauss waltz in Vienna or a Palestrina motet in the Sistine Chapel: sounds that came together in the mind with the taste of sweet tea and the sight of hulking, ancient forms in the landscape.

But as the verses came forth it was not the music but the black, ghostly figure of the minstrel himself that held me hypnotized. Sitting before me, hunched over the slender *saz*, the man seemed to personify all that I had brooded about in the last eight hours: the burned father on the train, the violence at the castle, Kemal's story of the tomb, and my own thoughts of Anatolia and its vanished wildlife. They all coalesced before me in this vision of self-destruction and pain, and gazing even more intently, I saw the dark form expand, fill my sight, and become not a man but a blurred embodiment of the land itself. The creases in his cheeks were the wadis etched boldly at sundown, and even as I watched, their shadows seemed to darken and retreat deeper into night. But in their depths I saw the moist crimson glint of something I had not seen before, and recognizing it I felt cold fear lay its hands upon me. For there, glistening darkly in the shadows, was the price of it all, the tribute poured out over the centuries, filling the cracked earth to overflowing. And the *saz* and the voice cried

We have paid enough,
Let us stop now,
Please stop,
Stop.

The next morning work resumed at the site. I was in charge of Julia, so I gave her a quick early morning tour of the castle before taking her back to the big tent, where she would be working with me on the pottery. At the castle site the peasants swarmed over the mounds of earth with their wheelbarrows and shovels. They were their usual stolid selves, working along as if the previous day's violence had never occurred. Kemal had received a delegation from the Kurdish village before work began. After apologizing, along with Sinan, for having let the matter get out of hand, he had once again tried to assure them of his continuing goodwill. The men had gone back to work, and as we stood on the north rampart looking down at them the two groups seemed indistinguishable from each other.

I took Julia to the north rampart because that was where we could get the best overall view of the operation. The castle sits on its rock like a triangle, and we stood at the apex facing the south gate and the mountain beyond. Clouds of swifts wheeled and darted over the limestone outcropping on which the castle was built. Behind us, the castle walls dropped fifty feet to the waters of Lake Tanyeri. Before us and to the left stood the palace and storehouse area. Our main efforts during previous campaigns had been directed there, and it was in the storehouses that we had found the giant tribute jars now lined up in the shed. We still had men digging there. The expedition's cluster of tents sat just beyond the storehouses in the southeast corner of the site. Slightly to the right of us, the Haldi temple had been roped off, plotted, and mapped, and was now methodically being stripped of its earth. Beyond the temple, in the southwest corner, dry grass and stones covered an area we hadn't yet touched, where we would start looking in the next year or two.

Julia and I walked toward the west side to get a closer look at the temple dig. Kemal, standing below with Sinan in the middle of the workers, waved up at us. They were at the far end, where the temple entrance had been. The workmen were removing the dirt starting from that point and working north toward us.

"Notice how the temple's entrance is oriented," I pointed out to Julia. "You see? It doesn't open straight south, the way it could, and it's not aligned with the palace walls either."

"I see! It's pointed right at the summit of the mountain."

"Exactly."

"What does it mean?"

"I couldn't say, really. Obviously the mountain must have some significance, but exactly what that is no one can say. Maybe we'll have to wait until someone locates and digs up

Musasir to find out. Maybe Haldi is some sort of mountain god. Who knows?"

"You said the temple was destroyed around 700 B.C. Was Tanyeri inhabited after that?"

"Yes, down to around 600. Urartu declined about that time, you see. The country was still under attack from all sides and gradually being infiltrated by the Armenians coming in from the west. After 600 B.C. there are no sites that can be identified as Urartian. The Armenians took over the plains, and the people of Urartu moved up to places like this in the mountains. From the mountains they kept a kind of guerrilla warfare going. That's what we think, anyway."

"So Tanyeri was inhabited for only two hundred years."

"By the Urartians anyway. Most of this castle was built later, probably by various local rulers: Armenians, Turks, and Kurds."

"What surprises me," said Julia, "is the size. I thought Tanyeri would be much bigger."

"No, it wasn't a big place. We think it was more of an outpost, close to the limits of Assyrian territory, from where the inhabitants could make raids toward the south. So there really weren't many people living here—maybe a thousand at the most."

"Still, that's more than the two villages have now."

"Yes, but the land must have been a lot richer then."

"How is that?"

"More trees, animals, better soil. They could probably afford to put their animals' manure back on the fields instead of burning it the way these people do now. You know, it's not because of the dry climate that these mountains are bare. It's because of the people."

Julia thought about that for a moment. "That's very sad," she said. "But somehow it manages to be beautiful anyway. In a different way."

66

"I know. Not beautiful like a girl but beautiful like an old woman. An old woman who has survived."

Julia soon fell in with our routine: up early, work all day, a swim in the afternoon, and the evening at the *çayhane.* The workers were making good progress in excavating the temple floor, though as yet we had not made any major discoveries. We were lucky to lose only one day of work, the Monday after Julia's arrival, when a brief, soaking rainstorm rolled in about midmorning and shook the tents for half an hour, ending digging for that day.

Julia and I talked a lot during those days. She told me about her marriage and the ironic way in which it had ended. I in turn told her about Kemal and me and the impasse we had reached. And I grew to like Julia very much. She was a beautiful woman with a slightly intimidating exterior, but upon closer acquaintance she revealed most of the same confusions that preoccupied me. She was a romantic, really. In the wake of divorce and disaster she had wandered to this valley and its mountain. The archaeology (as she freely admitted) had been an excuse to justify traveling to Hasan Gazi. Not that she wasn't interested in what we were doing; she was, and she did her work well, whether in pottery with me or helping out Kemal and the others. But it became obvious as the days rolled on toward August that a fever was growing in her to be off and away from our tents and potsherds and the endless wheelbarrows of dirt. She and Sinan began to take long hikes in the evening to toughen themselves up for the climb, and many times around sundown I would see her sitting alone or with Sinan on the south rampart of the castle staring at the mountain, as if in a trance.

A lot of things came together on Friday, the twentieth, ten days after Julia arrived, and a week before she planned to climb the mountain. Julia and I were working together that day. About ten o'clock Orhan rushed in and told us to come quickly to the temple. We followed and found Kemal and Sinan down in the pit supervising, along with Bekir Bey. Digging just inside what appeared to be the main sanctuary of the temple, the workmen had uncovered a massive sculptured stone some six feet long and two feet across at its widest point. Julia and I watched from the edge of the excavation as the stone gradually emerged from beneath its covering of dirt. The shape, however, was unmistakable: a giant spearhead, long, narrow, tapering very gradually to a point. Kemal looked up, smiling and laughing with excitement. "Recognize it?" he said to me.

"Of course! It's fantastic!"

"This may be just what we need to justify this campaign."

"What is it, for heaven's sake?" Julia asked.

"It must be one of the big stone spearheads that were set up inside the temple and also on top of it. We've seen pictures of them before in Assyrian reliefs, but this is the first we've ever actually dug up. It's an absolutely fantastic find!"

"Mary! Come down here! Look at this!" Kemal called up to me. I jumped into the pit just as the workers were very gingerly setting the stone down after having turned it over. It was an excellent piece of granite sculpture, perhaps six inches thick in the middle and tapering to a fine edge on either side. Miraculously, the stone had remained intact through the destruction of the temple.

"Look, Mary!" Kemal was pointing to a place down near the point. He and Bekir were talking to each other excitedly in Turkish. I pushed my way past one of the workers to get a closer look. Leaning over Kemal's shoulder I saw at last what he and Bekir were talking about. At the extreme end of the stone, within six inches of the point, an inscription had been chiseled in the neat, minuscule patterns of Assyrian cuneiform. It said "To thee, Haldi, my spear, my blood, my life. Rusa son of Sarduri."

Rusa son of Sarduri! It had to be Rusa II, king at the time of the Assyrian invasion and the sack of Musasir in 714 B.C. Did this mean that the temple had been built by Rusa himself? Had Tanyeri been a royal residence, perhaps a refuge during the turbulent years of Scythian, Cimmerian, and Assyrian attacks? Grounds for a lot of speculation, obviously. What a find! I could hardly contain myself. Neither could Kemal, Bekir, and the others, now happily talking among themselves in Turkish. Suddenly it looked like we might be getting somewhere.

At lunch that day we talked at length about the stone and its inscription. Bekir, typically cautious, would not say for certain that the king had built this particular temple. How could we know yet? Kemal was more hopeful, saying that at the very least it raised a host of interesting questions. Sinan, as might have been expected, was ready to declare that we had found Musasir and the second capital of the kingdom of Van, all from the discovery of the stone.

Almost immediately after lunch the cry went up again. More finds. Another granite spear point like the first, this one broken. Smaller items appeared: bronze fragments, bits of armor, a helmet inscribed to Haldi. And more rubble than we had ever unearthed before. It appeared that we had broken into an area where the remains of the holocaust lay thick upon the floor of the temple. Debris lay seemingly everywhere, and we as archaeologists reveled in it.

About three o'clock the yield from the temple seemed to be leveling off from those incredible few hours of the morning and early afternoon. By four o'clock we could see a definite lull in the digging. Julia and I decided to break early and go for our customary late afternoon swim. The voice of conscience told me to stay and see what else might be dug up from the temple, but my hot, dusty body said something quite different. We went over to the temple to see if Sinan or Frank wanted to come along, but both intended to stay on the job despite the heat.

We changed into our suits in the tent and took off on the path that leads down the east side of the castle. Julia led as usual, running nimbly down the steep, narrow pathway as if it were a broad and level boulevard. From the base of the castle rock we had only a short walk across a field and through a grove of poplars to a small beach where we usually swam.

The trees made it a very pleasant spot. There were two large stands of poplars, each planted in rigidly symmetrical ranks and shimmering in the sun like giant leafy telephone poles. The groves were separated by a dry stream bed whose sand and pebbles had washed down to form a tiny beach. This stream bed also delineated the boundary between Tanyeri and Gaziova territory. I liked swimming there. We had trees, a degree of privacy, and, of course, a magnificent view of the castle and the mountain overhead.

Arriving at the beach we shed our clothes and entered the water. It was so cold we could only bear it by plunging in quickly and swimming out into the lake very fast. We headed for a spot in the water that Julia had discovered the week before. She found that by swimming some fifty yards out and slightly toward the west she entered an area about ten yards in diameter where the water was, if not actually warm, at least quite bearable. We surmised that some sort of hot spring was active along the bottom, a remnant of the volcanism that once had produced Hasan Gazi.

I swam hard through the icy water toward the patch of warmth hidden somewhere in the ripples. It wasn't always easy to find; usually we could locate it by lining up with the castle and one of the trees onshore. But it shifted from day to day.

"Here it is!" Julia called out close on my left.

I swam several strokes toward her and suddenly felt the water's biting edge turn to a healing, restful coolness.

"Aaah . . . wonderful" I sighed, turning over on my back to look up at the sky.

"It's like coming out of the cold into a sauna."

We floated there for some seconds, the mountain looking down on us like a hoary, ancient god. No clouds remained from the rainstorm of three days before, and the cone was a dazzling, pure white.

"Just look at that!" said Julia. "Are you sure you don't want to come with us next week?"

"Quite sure," I said. "I'm content to stay down here and just look at it." Both of us were treading water now. The water felt even warmer on the tips of my toes.

"I guess that's not enough for me," Julia mused. "I want to be on it, a part of it."

"You want to see what's on the other side."

"Oh yes, that too. But—I was thinking about this last night, about why I came all this way—just for this, really. I think it's wanting to be part of such a beautiful thing. When you're up there it's wonderful, not only the view, but knowing that you're part of what people see when they look up at the mountain. Even though, of course, they can't really see you at all. You're lost in it. I think that's what I like about it.

"Besides," she said, the excitement fairly bursting from her, "maybe we will find something worth looking at. Maybe we'll see some more of that lost city Sinan always talks about."

I laughed. "Well, you and Sinan can go looking for it. Personally, I'm quite happy to stay here with Kemal and find out what's in the next cubic meter of dirt."

"Good for you," Julia laughed as she turned over on her back again. We lay drifting for some seconds in the island of warm water. It felt gorgeous. When Julia spoke next, she expressed my feelings exactly.

"I'm horny," she said.

I let out a yelp, partly of delight and partly because at that exact moment I had drifted out of the warm water. I was upright in a flash, treading water and giggling like a schoolgirl. Julia started swimming back to shore, and I followed. By the time we got back to shore the two of us were shivering and giggling our way into a state of total incoherence. A few minutes later we had toweled off and were sitting on the sand brushing our hair.

"Well?" Julia said.

"Well what?"

"Well, I said I was horny. Do you think I should mess around with our friend Sinan or not?"

"Why do you have to ask me?"

"Because you know the country. You know the people. You know Turkish men—one Turkish man anyway. What do you think?"

"I don't know."

"Well, say yes then."

"Why?"

"Because he's so pretty."

"Yes, he is, isn't he?" I laughed, imagining Sinan's exasperation if he were ever confronted with that adjective applied to himself. I thought about her question. I had seen the two of them go off on several early evening hikes proposed for the purpose of conditioning themselves. They looked very nice together, I had to admit. But then they looked very nice separately also.

"Actually," I said, "my answer would be no."

Julia stopped brushing her hair for a minute and looked at me. "Why?" she said.

"Because I don't think he could handle it. Because I'm sure he'd fall in love with you."

"Yes, he would, wouldn't he?" It wasn't a boast, simply a statement of fact. She put her brush away and stared off across the lake. "And for my last week in Tanyeri I would have a very possessive young man following me around."

"Yes, you would."

She thought a moment longer. "He's very nice, though, isn't he?"

"Yes."

"Very intelligent."

"Yes."

"Kind . . . but basically dull."

I laughed. "Yes."

Smiling softly, Julia continued to gaze at the water. "You know," she said, "it's sad to say that about someone like Sinan. I want to like him, to be turned on by him. But he is dull. Maybe he's better with Turkish girls. Yes! We'll give him the benefit of the doubt and say it's the language barrier."

"But he speaks excellent English."

"True. So much for that excuse. Don't worry, though, Mary. If I do commit an indiscretion I will be very discreet about it."

"It doesn't matter, I'm sure."

"Why not?"

"I'm sure the workmen all think you're sleeping with him anyway."

"Oh!"

"That's the way people think around here. You're a whore until proved otherwise, and there's no way you will ever prove you're not one."

"Really?"

"Yes. When Kemal and I began our affair three summers ago I used to worry all the time about being found out. Then one night Kemal said, 'Stop worrying, Mary. In Turkey they think every foreign woman is a whore anyway. These peasants can't possibly think any worse of you than they do, so stop worrying.' I was really shocked when he said that. Everyone had been so kind up until then. They still are. I couldn't figure it out."

"But how could both things be true?"

"I'm not sure. I guess it's because I'm a foreigner, and the rules of hospitality remove me from their control. But if I ever got into trouble, if I ever did anything that brought me within their jurisdiction, I don't like to think about what might happen."

"So all this talk about the wonderful hospitality . . . ?"

"No," I broke in, "I don't mean to say it's a sham or anything like that. I've known too much kindness in this country *ever* to say such a thing. But still I'm a woman, and I worry sometimes."

Shrill, distant laughter interrupted our conversation.

"Look!" Julia said, pointing behind me toward the east.

I turned around and then smiled at what I saw. A quarter of a mile away a group of Kurdish women and girls was wading into the water in their bright, baggy trousers and blouses, squealing at the shock of the cold water, splashing each other, laughing and shouting. It was a familiar sight to me: always amusing, but a bit sad as well to know that they would always be wading, not swimming, and all the time wearing the only clothes they owned.

"Let's go and say hello," said Julia.

I hesitated. I've always been a bit shy about meeting people, and anyway I wanted to get back to the castle.

"All right. I don't know if I can speak to them though."

"Why not?"

"They probably speak only Kurdish. Never mind, let's try anyway."

We finished dressing and began to walk east down the shoreline toward the women. They saw us coming almost immediately, and from a distance I could see their bright scarves and blouses flashing colorfully as they pointed and twittered excitedly to each other.

"Look at them!" Julia exclaimed.

"Yes, they're wonderful. Now we know how Columbus felt."

The women, some ten in number, stood open-mouthed and wide-eyed as we walked up. Wreathed in eager smiles, their faces proclaimed us the wonder of the age. They were like children surprised on the playground by a visit from the principal.

One of the older women greeted us in Kurdish, and the others followed in a chorus. Figuring that they must have said "welcome," I gave the proper reply in Turkish and asked if any of them spoke that language. One did, a very handsome woman whose strong brown features had not yet been ruined by her life in the fields, though deep wrinkles had already formed around her eyes and across her forehead. Like the others she wore a bright scarf over her black, braided hair, a loose-fitting, brightly colored blouse, and cotton trousers so loose and billowy that they appeared to be a skirt at first glance.

I asked the woman where she had learned Turkish. She said she had lived in Bitlis many years before as a child. Her playmates had spoken Turkish, and she had learned it also in school, which she had attended for two years. I asked if she could read or write, and she said she could write her name. She eagerly volunteered to show us her unusual skill. (I'm sure she must have been the only woman in her village who could write.) I had nothing to write with, but Julia dug a ballpoint and a scrap of paper out of her bag. One of the younger girls donated her back for a writing surface, and the woman went to work, slowly forming the letters with great effort, her weathered hands straining to remember what they had learned years ago. The woman finished and triumphantly handed me the paper. It said LATIFE. I told Latife I was pleased to meet her and introduced myself and Julia. The other women were talking and laughing. Latife was obviously very proud of herself. She asked me to write down my name and Julia's. When I did, she took the paper and slowly read them back to me. She was having a wonderful time, and I loved her.

After that the women started inspecting us. They asked us our country, and we told them. Through Latife they asked about our blue jeans, our tennis shoes, our bags—how much did they cost, where did we get them? They were especially interested in Julia's blond hair. Was it real or dyed, they asked. (At that point one of the women displayed her hair, dyed with henna.) They asked if we were married and were baffled to find that we were not. I told them that Julia's husband had died, and they clicked their tongues in sympathy. Then they asked why she wasn't in mourning, and that took some time to explain. Latife said Julia's husband must have paid much money for such a beautiful woman, and again I had to make a long explanation about American marriage practices. They listened open-mouthed and uncomprehending. Latife asked me how old Julia and I were. When I told her Julia was thirty she couldn't believe it. She herself was only twenty-five, although she looked closer to thirty-five going on forty. Her hands looked fifty. She asked if Julia had any children. What! No children? She had four, she said proudly.

We had a wonderful time asking each other questions and looking each other over. But after fifteen minutes of talking we had to say good-bye, for it was well after five, and I wanted to see if anything more had happened at the site.

It was the simple act of turning and walking away that brought on the mood. We walked along the shoreline, crunching the pebbles underfoot. And I could feel my spirits plummet from the height of gaiety and laughter we had experienced only moments before.

I hadn't seen much of the local women during my three summers at Tanyeri. They were kept away, remote and inaccessible, visible only at their daily labors in the fields. I had, however, met groups of them before in situations such as this one along the lakeshore, and I always marveled at how cheerful they managed to be. Not that it proved anything. Somehow people manage to laugh no matter how miserable their circumstances. But uttering the cliché is nothing compared to seeing it before you: real human beings emerging from behind the wall of custom and poverty, managing to find pleasure at your slightest gesture or word.

"Weren't they wonderful?!" I said.

"Yes, they were. Beautiful too."

"Very beautiful."

"You know," Julia mused sadly as we walked into the late afternoon sun, "two minutes ago I was laughing and talking with ten beautiful women, and now I could almost cry."

"I know," I said, "I feel the same way."

Five minutes' walk brought us to the small beach where we had been swimming only half an hour before. By this time I felt restless, eager to return to the moral neutrality of objects dug out of the earth and tagged for future study. With Julia leading the way, we took the path that angled off into the shadows of the poplar grove. The trees were big at that end of the grove, a foot thick and more, standing tall in their long, symmetrical rows. The ranks pressed in on either side of the path, leaving barely enough space for two people to pass through.

Julia walked about ten yards in front of me, her shoulder bag swinging softly against her left hip. Swirls and patches of late afternoon light filtered through the swaying branches and cascaded over our bodies as we ambled along. Overhead the leaves rustled in the breeze.

Fifty yards ahead, at the point where the path emerged into a sunlit field, the dark silhouette of a man appeared carrying a scythe in his left hand. Seeing us, he paused for a second, then walked on. My mind by this time had locked into the idea of "home": the tent, the temple, supper, and a shower. Aware only of the trees and the beaten path unrolling at my feet I was indifferent to the sight of another gray-clad peasant walking home at day's end. So when I looked up and saw the man approaching Julia and felt the hollow nausea in my throat that told me *this isn't right, this isn't right—look at his eyes,* it was too late, and the scream I tried to bring forth stuck like mucus in my throat.

As Julia and the peasant met in the narrow path she moved to the left to let him pass. To no purpose. In a movement so swift I did not really see it the man's hand reached out, grabbed Julia's right breast, and shoved her brutally against the trunk of the nearest poplar. Julia gasped in shock while I struggled to produce what only came out an inarticulate, impotent cry of rage. The peasant turned to face me, and for a fleeting instant I looked into the eyes of a man who could have ripped me open without thinking twice. The image burned in my mind for an instant, electric with hate and terror. Then he was gone, walking down the path in the same hulking way as before.

"Are you all right?" I managed to blurt out.

"Yes," Julia answered in a hoarse whisper. "Yes, I'm all right." She leaned against the tree trunk, head bowed and hair hanging loose in front of her face. We were both breathing heavily. Though she was unhurt—except for possible bruises and a button missing on her blouse—and though the whole incident had taken no more than five seconds, Julia could not have been more thoroughly and brutally violated if she had been assaulted by a gang. Inside me I felt the aftermath of fear harden into anger. I clenched my teeth and sobbed.

"Stop it!" Julia hissed at me. "Stop it! That's just what that bastard wants!"

I didn't stop. "That's just what he deserves, too," I sobbed. "Hatred. The very best hatred I've got." To hell with stoicism. I hated anybody who would do what he had done, and I felt like showing it.

We stayed there in shadows for several minutes, trembling like the poplar leaves overhead.

"Come on," Julia breathed hoarsely, "let's get out of here."

I wiped my eyes on my sleeve. "All right," I said, and followed her down the path. Even above the rustling of the poplars I could hear my teeth grinding together.

We were trudging up the east side of the citadel rock when one of the workers appeared on the wall above and yelled down at us.

"*Mary Hanim! Gel! Çabuk çabuk!*"

"*Ne için? Ne oldu?*"

"*Gel! Güzel bir şey bulduk!*"

"What is he saying?" Julia asked.

"He says they've found something."

"Oh." She didn't change speed.

"I'd better go look." I hurried past her and up the last few feet to the top, then ran past the tents to the temple area. It was after 5:30, but the workers were still there, gathered around the pit. The sun floated yellow above the rim of mountains in the west.

As I came closer I saw Kemal, who waved to me with an excited and happy smile on his face. He was standing inside the excavation along with Sinan, Frank, Bekir Bey, and Orhan. Mahmut was on the west side taking pictures. The air pulslated with excited talk in Turkish.

"Mary, come and look!" Kemal exclaimed.

I broke through the crowd of workmen gathered around the edge and climbed into the pit. I saw what Kemal was pointing to. Skeletons. Four of them close together in a circle, sprawled in various attitudes on the temple floor. I bent down for a closer look, marveling at the find. The bones were gray, but inside each of the skulls I could see the black remnants of brains, carbonized long ago by the holocaust. Several had metal bracelets on their wrists, and each held a small black lump of metal clenched in its bony fingers.

"They're wonderful! When did you find them?" I asked.

"Around five o'clock. We came upon the first one just before the men were going to leave. Then the second one turned up and the third and the fourth—all within the next half hour."

"It's incredible!" I said. I walked around behind him to look at the others. I was transported. "What are these lumps of metal they're holding?"

"Look closely," Kemal said.

I picked one up and held it. It seemed to have no shape at all. Then I looked at one of the others, and from the angle at which it lay I recognized the form—the flanks, the maned head.

"Of course! They're lions! Very crude and decayed, but definitely lions."

80

"What do they mean?" Julia asked. She had appeared above us standing at the edge of the excavation, surrounded by the workmen with their shovels. She looked very tired.

"The lion is the symbol of Haldi," I answered. "They've found reliefs at other sites showing Haldi on the back of a lion."

"So who were these people?"

"We think they were priestesses," said Kemal.

"Priestesses? How do you know?" Julia asked quietly.

"Well, obviously we don't know for certain. We only discovered them an hour ago. But from spot measurements we have taken—pelvic measurements—they appear to be women. They are wearing jewelry. And they are all holding these small bronze lions."

"The symbol of the god," Julia said.

"Yes," Kemal continued, "so they must have had something to do with the temple."

"Priestesses, you say."

"Yes, probably."

"Or temple prostitutes?"

"That is also possible, I suppose."

"Then what happened to them?"

"Well, let's look at the evidence. We know that the temple was destroyed in an attack. A Scythian attack. We have rubble everywhere: charcoal fragments, Scythian arrowheads, charred beams. And now four skeletons, grouped together and each holding a bronze lion. They must have been killed in the attack."

"Yes," Julia said simply. She looked down at the four skeletons with a troubled look on her face. She opened her mouth to speak, hesitated, then asked, "Have you found any other skeletons left from the Scythian attack?"

Kemal looked puzzled and said "No, not yet. Why do you ask?"

"The palace area and the storehouses all showed evidence of destruction in this attack, didn't they?"

"Yes, they did."

"But you didn't find any bodies there?"

"No, we didn't. I don't quite understand...."

It seemed suddenly very quiet. Everyone was listening to her questions, even those who could not understand. The dying sun shed its soft light on Julia, on the blond hair hanging loose around her face, and on the brown, eroded faces of the peasants who stood beside her. Above them the mountain, silent beneath its mantle of snow.

Julia spoke haltingly, almost painfully. "What I mean is, why are these the only bodies that have been found?" She paused, frowning intently at the skeletons sprawled against the brown earth. "Why were these only ones left? Did the other people surrender?"

"Perhaps. We don't know."

"Were the others given funerals, do you suppose?"

"How can we know?"

"Why did they die?" She asked the question quietly, of no one in particular, staring all the while at the skeletons.

I followed her gaze and looked down again at the bones sprawled before me. Like Julia I slowly began to perceive them not as the neutral artifacts my professional eyes had seen minutes before, but as the earthly remnants of human beings. And seeing them as human beings, I too had to ask the questions that absorbed Julia. What *were* these four women doing here? Why had they stayed inside the building? Had they been unable to flee? Or unwilling? *Unwilling?* Why? Why did they die like this, clutching the amulet of an extinct and useless god? Why?

I could find no answer. I looked up again at Julia, feeling dizzy from the emotions and questions whirling in my head. I was sorry to have come back to this mystery lying in the dirt. As Julia stood above us the breeze blew a lock of yellow hair across the opening in her blouse where the button had been ripped away. She lifted her eyes from the skeletons and looked at me. For the most fleeting instant our eyes locked in a bond of ineffable sadness. Julia started to speak, then stopped and looked away. At the corners of her mouth there flickered the intimations of a smile.

Julia
Warren

My last week in Tanyeri, the week I had been antici- pating for so long, began with the Kurban Bayram on Mon- day, July 23. Kemal informed me that Kurban Bayram means the "Feast of the Sacrifice" and commemorates the biblical story of Abraham and Isaac. In case you don't remember (I didn't—Sunday school was long ago), Isaac was spared ex- ecution on the condition that Abraham sacrifice a sheep to Jehovah every year on that day. Today the god is Allah, and the peasants are Turks, but the sheep are still sacrificed—in droves.

The week before I had been just as eager to attend this feast as I had been to set off up the mountain, but after Fri- day's incident in the poplars I was none too anxious to walk into the village and have to face that man again. Kemal had apologized and assured me that the man was probably from the other village, but by Monday I was positively feverish with the desire to hoist my pack and climb out of this valley and up into the snow.

Monday afternoon I felt edgy as we walked across the fields toward Tanyeri village. Everybody was off, of course, this being one of the biggest religious holidays of the year. We, the mighty team of archaeologists, were out in full force for the occasion. Even Bekir Bey and Mahmut, our lovable bookworms, had emerged from behind their trays of artifacts and were striding in the lead, busily discussing what was no doubt a very urgent archaeological problem. As usual I was walking with Sinan, but there was nothing usual about his behavior. Normally we would talk about archaeology, or more often about trivia. But today Sinan was revealing a new aspect—a politically opinionated and anti-American aspect that had not surfaced before. He started by talking about antiquities smuggling, which he said was being aided and abetted by the Central Intelligence Agency. Then he went on to discuss the tragedy and injustice of the ban on opium cultivation. He finished with an account of present-day political repression and the opinion that the CIA, in league with American business, was exploiting Turkey and manipulating its politicians to their advantage. I told him how glad I was to hear about all of this.

"Yes," he said, "you should be informed of what your government is doing."

"No, I meant I was glad to hear that the U.S. government is handling things so well over here."

"What do you mean?" he said, looking befuddled.

"Well," I said, "they can't seem to run anything right in the States. It's good to hear that they're so competent and well-organized in Turkey. Imagine being able to manipulate the affairs of a nation of 35 million people. It's marvelous. I'm beginning to have faith in my own government again."

Sinan considered this for a moment.

"I do not think this is a good thing for Turkey," he said. Sinan wasn't stupid, just terribly *earnest*.

"No, it's not a good thing, if it's true."

"It is true!"

"Yes. All right."

"Why don't you believe me?"

"I do believe you." I wanted to change the subject.

"No, you don't believe me. You think your government is so much better than ours." He said this with massive sarcasm.

"Ha! It's precisely because I think our government is so clumsy that I said what I said. I mean, how can they be so great at controlling Turkey when they can't even run the United States half the time?"

He didn't answer, so I went on.

"Really, Sinan, I think you ought to be grateful to the United States."

"Grateful! For what? For your spies stationed here? For your capitalists exploiting us and taking our money? We don't need you!"

"No, for our target value."

"What?"

"I mean, if you didn't have the CIA to blame for your troubles, what would you do? You might have to do something about them."

"Come on, Julia," Mary broke in, "that's not exactly fair is it?"

"I suppose not, but look: was that a CIA man who attacked me last Friday? Is it the CIA that sells your women like cattle? Was it a CIA team that chopped down all the trees in Turkey? Is it the CIA that owns these villages and lives in Ankara?"

"The CIA supports the reactionary government that keeps these people in power!" Sinan was red in the face by this time.

"Yes, and I suppose it was the CIA that voted that government into power."

"Stop it!" Kemal broke in. "Enough politics! This is a feast day."

I started laughing at this point. It's so much fun being nationalistic occasionally. Helps to clear the blood from the strain of being liberal and "understanding" all the time. My edginess had gone. I smiled my very best smile at Sinan, and he managed a weak, conciliatory smile in return.

Ahead, a chorus of dogs announced that we were coming closer to the village. Beneath their barking I could hear the insistent beat of a bass drum.

I glanced again at Sinan walking beside me. The violence of his anti-Americanism had surprised me. *He certainly had kept his politics well hidden,* I thought. *Always something seething beneath the surface in these people. Like that fight the first day I came here. Bang! It exploded, and then we heard nothing more about it. And that man in the grove . . . no, I don't want to think about that.*

Three of the village sheepdogs appeared and hovered five yards away on either side of us, snarling and showing their teeth. The trick here, I had been taught, is not to be friendly or unfriendly, to do nothing in fact, but keep walking. Above all, I had been told not to stop and look at them or I might risk losing an arm. Ahead of me, Kemal and Mary were following their own advice, but I couldn't resist glancing to the side now and then at the magnificent gray dogs, barely evolved from wolves. Each wore a black metal collar bristling with spikes. I kept on walking.

We were on the road coming into Tanyeri from the east. Above the drum's throbbing I could hear the reedy wail of a pipe: raw, exotic music. And then voices, laughing and shouting, mixed together over the ferocious threats of the dogs. We walked into the village past the piles of dung cakes and the houses dug into the side of the hill. A donkey wandered about, and several chickens pecked in the dust. At last a man walked out of a house ahead, and spying us came forward to say welcome. I recognized him as one of the workers at the castle, a bearded old man who always wore the most outrageously patched trousers on the job. Today he was without patches. The old man shook hands with us, then picked up several rocks and hurled them at the dogs, who barked as ferociously as ever. They didn't retreat an inch.

Once in the village square we found ourselves surrounded by people welcoming us and shaking our hands. Kemal and Bekir had become important men in this town. They employed about half the adult male population. Many of these men gathered around to shake our hands and guide us to a place in the shade of the big tree that dominated the square. There, across from the teahouse, they had set out tables and chairs for us, the guests of honor. The villagers sat on rugs and mats laid out on the stones.

Across the square, directly in front of the teahouse, four men with linked hands danced in slow, dignified cadence to the bass drum and the wailing oboe. Everywhere I looked there were large round platters of food. They may have starved the rest of the year, but today they were eating. In a matter of seconds the platters started coming our way, all carried by women each of whom literally pleaded with us to take something from her particular tray. There was lamb, pilaf made from bulgur wheat, stuffed tomatoes, stuffed peppers, stuffed zucchini, stuffed eggplant. I stuffed myself.

About twenty people watched us eat—men, women, and round-eyed children. I felt as if I were on display in a Family-Life-in-Ancient-Times exhibit at the Museum of Natural History in reverse. The people from ancient times were looking at me.

Soon the questions began. One old woman with a white scarf wrapped low on her forehead said something in a high, piercing voice. Sinan, sitting on my left, translated.

"This woman asked why we are going to climb the mountain."

"What! How does she know we're going to climb the mountain?"

"They know. They know everything that goes on."

"Oh. Well, tell them we're climbing it because it's there."

"What?"

"Because it's there." Mary laughed, dear girl. She at least has a sense of humor.

"I can't translate that into Turkish."

"Then tell them we're doing it for fun."

"They'll never believe that."

"Then tell them we're crazy."

"I think they will believe that." Sinan turned to the assembled group and translated this last remark. It got a big laugh. Then one of the men, slightly taller than the others and better dressed, spoke up and asked another question.

"He wants to know if we are searching for minerals."

"Minerals?! What minerals?"

"Gold, silver."

"Why does he think that?"

"I think they have seen your ice axe."

"They do know everything, don't they?"

"They have seen us hiking."

Sinan explained to the man what my ice axe was for.

"Sinan," I said, "ask them if anyone from their village has climbed the mountain."

It didn't take much knowledge of Turkish to see that the answer was no.

"They have never gone. They say, 'Why? We have enough snow in winter. We do not need snow in summer.' "

A swarthy little man with a very thick moustache leaned over the table and asked Frank a question, pointing to me as he did so. When he heard the question Sinan started laughing.

"What did he say?" Frank asked, chewing on a piece of lamb.

"Ha! He wants to know if you are Julia's father."

"Her father!" Frank laughed. "He doesn't know much about heredity, does he? Does he think this is a paint job I've got?"

"I don't know, but he asks what is your price for Julia."

"What!" I almost gagged on my pilaf.

"He wants to buy you for his wife. Don't worry, he is only ninety percent serious."

"Oh, charming." I looked at the man. He was serious all right. He looked as if he had just made an offer on a new sheep. Sinan declined the proposal on my behalf.

After this, another woman asked if Sinan and I were betrothed. They had seen us walking together and assumed we were. And on it went, an endlessly unwinding skein of questions for Frank and me that stretched out over the next hour. What is your job? How much money do you make? (Much explaining of our *embarras de richesses*.) Is America beautiful? Is America rich? How much do brides cost in America? Are you married? If you are a widow, why don't you wear black? Do you have children? What is your religion? How can God be three people to Christians? Do you believe that Jesus is the son of God? Is Jesus in heaven? Are there Muslims in America? Are there Turks in America? Does America have mountains? Are there donkeys in America? Is the water good in America? In Turkey the water is wonderful. Is the soil good in America? Here it is stones. Wasn't Kennedy a great man? Who killed Kennedy? Johnson? Why did Mrs. Kennedy marry a *Yunan*? Why is America the friend of the *Yunans*? Will you take me to America? Is it far? Where is America? Is it west or east? Is America bigger than Turkey? Are there many schools in America? Do you like Turkey? Turkey is beautiful, yes?

There was no time for me to feel uneasy with these people. They were so open and inquisitive and eager to talk to anyone out of the ordinary that self-consciousness became impossible. I was astounded. Mary sat on my right placidly eating her food, occasionally laughing at a question or my perplexity in answering it. Sinan barely had a chance to eat, what with all the translating he was called upon to do. And all this time the music wailed on as a group of men, sometimes only three, sometimes as many as seven, danced in a row, their arms on each other's shoulders, dipping and swaying to the rhythm laid down by the man with the drum.

Between questions my eyes would sweep around to the right through the dusty square swarming with noise and people and rest on the white hump of Hasan Gazi rising high over the mud roofs of the village. And as I gazed I daydreamed again about this mountain and why it seemed to mean so much more to me than to these peasants. *What is it to them?* I asked myself. *A mountain that sits there, one of many mountains, a part of the earth. A bit higher, perhaps, but part of the same earth that we plow. Yes, it is beautiful. But a god? A divine presence? No, they would say, it's just a mountain.*

Obviously something had changed in those centuries since the rulers of Urartu built a temple to Haldi and oriented its doorway toward the summit of the volcano. At some point the mountain had lost its magic in the minds of the dwellers beneath it. Now it hung there like a picture stuck up on a wall and forgotten. To these people, Hasan Gazi meant nothing.

But having said that, the opposite thought came storming forth from another section of my mind. *Don't be stupid, Julia. That mountain is something to these people; it is, in fact, everything. Without its melting snow they couldn't sur-*

94

vive. Their fruit trees, their vegetables, and their sheep would all die within a season.

But why, I argued with myself, *don't any of them climb it or even look at it the way I am looking at it now?*

You know why, Julia. Because they live with it, and you come only as a consumer. Long after you've returned to your suburban heaven and told a hundred times the story of your mountain in Turkey they'll still be here. As they burrow into their houses, they'll watch the snow gather again in winter and the lake freeze solid. And then in summer the snow will retreat again toward the crater. They know this mountain and are thankful for it in a hundred ways that you could never dream of back in New Canaan. But think, on Friday morning you will stand on top in the wind and view the mountains of four nations. For what? For the experience, for the joy, yes. And also for that memory you can store away and fondle like a dainty gold charm, a memory without which—who knows?—you might not like yourself quite so much. Then look at these people and consider. Self-respect to them isn't something fourteen thousand feet in the air half a world away. It's right there, in the dust of the square, in those feet lifting and falling with the music, in the eyes of those men drinking tea in the shade. You can see that, can't you?

Of such stuff was the afternoon made.

The next day I began to get everything organized for the beginning of the climb on Wednesday. As he had hoped, Kemal managed to borrow sleeping bags and rucksacks from the local military gendarmes, one of each for both Sinan and Frank, whom we had finally persuaded to come along. The sleeping bags were old U.S. Army-issue, feather-filled mummies, a bit ratty, but serviceable. Equally serviceable, though very heavy, were the large canvas rucksacks. I figured that the two men, lacking ice axes, would need something to walk with, so on Tuesday afternoon Sinan and I went to the village and bought two straight white poplar staffs from a man who had hundreds of them in many lengths and diameters stacked like organ pipes in front of his shop. With one end whittled to a point they were the best walking staffs we could get. For a walk-up like Hasan Gazi, with no glaciers to speak of, I was reluctant to bother with any kind of rope. But having brought a 120-foot perlon rope all the way from home I felt ridiculous leaving it behind. So in the end I decided to take it. Another four pounds to carry. For food I had brought along several packaged concoctions from Instant America: freeze-dried chicken with rice, instant oatmeal, and soup. To that we added a lot of stuff from the expedition larder, including some heavily salted white cheese and a bundle of the thin, flexible unleavened peasant bread that Sinan said was called *yufka*, which I had eaten at Monday's feast. Lying in great piles next to the food, the bread had looked very much like old, unused newsprint. I regret to say that it had approximately the same flavor: that is, none at all. It had, however, the advantages of being filling, nutritious, and compact. Together, the *yufka* and the white cheese seemed likely to induce instant colonic concretion. And, heaven help us, we might need it.

After considerable discussion we had decided upon a plan of assault that placed a minimum of strain on our admittedly tender bodies. It seemed the best plan, physically as well as aesthetically, to go slowly to get acclimatized. We planned to start right after lunch on Wednesday and camp somewhere short of the tomb that night. Thursday called for a late rising, a hike up to the tomb, and an early camp somewhere above it. On Friday morning, July 27, we would head for the top at dawn. We expected to be back by the middle of the afternoon.

Tuesday night we gathered in the headquarters tent to look at the maps and get everything settled for the next day. There were five of us in the tent: Kemal, Mary, Sinan, Frank, and I. A round propane cylinder sat like a silver pumpkin at one corner of the table and hissed as its mantle, a white blob of light, glowed inside the glass window. We were a romantic-looking crew, I must say, Kemal puffing on his pipe, Mary standing tall and lovely beside him, and Frank a black mountain of strength at the far end of the table. Standing beside me in the glow of the lamp Sinan looked even more handsome than usual. Kemal had unfolded the map upside down on the table with Hasan Gazi, which lay to the south of us, at the top of the paper. As mapped, the mountain was a very impressive gathering of contour lines that flowed together and culminated in a tiny cross at the center reading, "4265 metre." Under the summit on the mountain's north face several contour lines blurred to form a solid line of black running east and west along the crest. This was the summit rampart Sinan had spoken of. It appeared from the contours to be about seventy-five feet high. Below it and to the left, on the mountain's northeast slope, another smaller circle of contour lines identified the secondary crater, where we would find the tomb of Hasan Gazi. It was all there before us. I was very excited.

"Now where is the trail we take?" I asked.

"Here." Kemal pointed to a broken line that wandered up the mountainside. "It follows the stream bed most of the way, then cuts through it and comes to a fork." He indicated a place where the dotted line split in two directions, one going right toward the west slope and the other, the one we wanted, toward the east.

"It looks easy enough," Frank observed.

"It is," Kemal agreed. "There is only one place where you might get confused. Right here." His finger rested on an area around the secondary crater where myriad tiny squiggles and markings indicated a complex topographical area.

"What is it?" I asked.

"I don't know what a geologist would make of it," said Kemal, "but to me it looked like a lava flow or igneous intrusions that were left standing alone by erosion. I don't know. At any rate there's a maze of very large rocks and boulders all over that side of the mountain. The path becomes very narrow and you can't see the summit. But if you just remember to keep going up, the path will come out by the crater. It really shouldn't be much of a problem."

"Is that why there are no shepherds up there?" I asked.

"Yes. As you can see, it would be impossible to keep a flock of sheep together in those rocks. They would make excellent hiding places for wolves."

"What about beyond the tomb?"

"That I don't know. From there on up you find your own path."

"Or ask directions," said Frank, smiling.

Sinan laughed. "Not very likely on that side of Hasan Gazi," he said.

"On the contrary," Kemal rejoined, "it is quite likely. I am certain you will meet some people at least. Remember, there is the tomb. There might be people there."

"Really?" I didn't know if I wanted that or not.

"It is possible. Also I remember seeing fields."

"Fields? They grow crops up there?"

"Yes, we saw two or three small wheatfields in the rocks, each about half the size of a tennis court."

"Incredible. That's not much bigger than my living room."

"You know, the city people in Turkey always say the peasants are lazy. 'They don't want to work,' they say. But I wonder how many people anywhere, in any country, would go that high to harvest grain from a field that size."

"In the States they wouldn't walk that far over level ground to buy a loaf of bread," Frank observed.

"They would if they were starving," I said.

"Or if they were crazy," Sinan added with a sly resplendent smile.

"You're so right, Sinan." And this time we both smiled.

At last, at noon on Wednesday, we began the climb, away from the castle, the dusty trenches, and the white canvas tents baking in the sun. Kemal and Mary, as well as many of the workmen, waved good-bye as the three of us marched out of the south gate of the castle. In the fields below the village the peasants were winnowing grain, tossing it into the wind again and again. I know they were all wondering why we were bothering with this insane project. I couldn't have done anything else with a mountain like this one beckoning. *Higher,* it said. *Come up here and dream.* Looking at it I could have wept for joy.

Half an hour later we were marching straight toward the summit over a barren plateau crisscrossed with goat tracks and broken occasionally by tiny fenced-in plots of ground where wheat had recently been harvested. The sun was very hot, and the early exhilaration of the climb had begun to wear off. We were all sweating freely and beginning to appreciate the grueling climb that lay ahead. I had the biggest and heaviest pack, but with its padded straps and waistbelt I was doing far better than Sinan and Frank with their canvas rucksacks.

As we walked uphill the entire landscape seemed to expand before our eyes. Ahead, the white cone of Hasan Gazi loomed larger and more intimidating than ever, as if gazing down in icy contempt at the sweating humans below. Looking back toward the receding village and the citadel, I noticed the lake seemed to shrink even farther into its trough among the mountains. Except for a cow far below us and the scarab beetles that pushed their balls of dung along the trail, we were the only living things in sight on that vast landscape of earth, rock, water, and snow.

Around four o'clock we arrived at the end of the trail that had been leading more or less straight up the face of the mountain. There the path branched off in two directions, one going to the left and to the east ridge, the other leading to the west. Up to that point we had been climbing through the bare plateau. There at the trail's turning we could see that the landscape before us had begun to change subtly. Above this place large black outcrops studded the brown earth of the mountain, breaking the monotony of the smooth slope. The rocks, some rounded and others squared off and jagged, must have been left over from the mountain's ancient period of activity. They lay strewn about like gigantic black grave markers in a long-neglected cemetery.

There was a large monolithic outcrop just beyond the place where the trail split, and in a depression on its shady east side we stopped to rest. Ahead of us the trail quickly disappeared among the rocks, while below the lake had shrunk to a tiny pool of silver lying at the base of the barren slope. Both Tanyeri and Gaziova had disappeared behind a fold of land.

I took off my pack and propped it against the rock. Frank brought out one of the canteens while I rummaged in a side pocket for some chocolate. We all sat down in the shade of the rock, facing up the trail. We had been marching for four hours through the hottest part of the day, and were beginning to tire. Frank took a swig from the canteen and passed it on.

"That stuff's almost warm," he said. "When are we going to find some water?"

"There's supposed to be water at a couple of places between here and the tomb," I said. "That's what the map says. Chocolate anyone?"

"Oh yes."

Sinan took some, and so did Frank. We munched on the chocolate squares and savored our weariness for a moment.

"Anyway I think the worst is over," Sinan said, looking down at the empty slopes we had just traversed.

"Yes," Frank agreed, "at least we'll have a few rocks to look at from now on."

"How is everybody doing?" I asked.

"I think I am getting a sore on my foot," Sinan said.

"You mean a blister?"

"No, it is not a blister."

"Not yet, you mean. I've got some moleskin in my pack. I'll put some on it." I started looking in the pack for my medical stuff.

"No, leave it. I don't want anything. If I leave it it will get strong."

"If you leave it you won't be able to walk the day after tomorrow."

"Leave it. It will be okay."

"Sinan, don't be such a fool." I found the moleskin and some scissors.

"Well, Sinan may not want some, but I think I could use it," Frank said. He took off his shoes and I cut a small section of the moleskin for him.

"Are you sure you don't want a piece, Sinan?" I asked.

"No, I don't need it."

"All right, suit yourself. But I don't want to hear you complaining on Friday morning."

"I will not complain!" he announced rather angrily.

"All right, all right," I said cutting off a couple of squares of moleskin for my own use. I might as well have accused him of being a Greek.

Sinan lifted his head and looked up the trail. Two peasants and a donkey had emerged from the rocks and were walking toward us. The donkey's back was piled high with newly cut wheat that must have come from one of the tiny fields Kemal had described and we had now seen. The man leading the donkey carried a long musketlike rifle cradled in his left arm while with his right he tugged on a rope attached to the animal's snout. His partner followed along behind, poking the donkey's rump occasionally with a stick that he held in his right hand. In his left hand he carried a long-handled scythe. They were typical Turkish peasants, short, swarthy, with thick moustaches, and what looked like about three days' growth of beard on their faces. In their dark clothes, dusty shoes, and flat caps, they seemed to have grown right out of the earth or been molded from the black rock along the trail. They halted a few feet short of our rock, and Sinan rose to greet them.

"*Selâm aleykum.*"

"*Aleykum selâm.*"

They started talking. The man with the rifle carried on most of the conversation, while his friend behind frowned skeptically at Frank and me. I finished applying the patches of moleskin to my nascent blisters and began putting on my shoes and socks again.

"What are you talking about, Sinan?" Frank asked.

"He wants to know who we are and where we're going."

"Who are they?"

"They are Kurds. From Gaziova."

"Ask them if there is water up ahead."

Sinan asked and the rifleman answered affirmatively. He gave a short explanation complete with gestures.

"He says there is water about an hour from here. He says to look for a stick pushed into the ground. The spring is up in the rocks to the right."

"Ask him how far to the tomb." The answer was, three or four hours.

"Are there people at the tomb?" The man said something and shrugged his shoulders.

"He does not know." The peasant added something else. "He says there are wolves. We should be careful."

"Wolves don't scare me. I hope we see some."

"He says they are dangerous."

"Only to sheep."

"He says we should have a gun." The peasant dropped the reins to his donkey and brandished the rifle for us. He was obviously proud of it. It looked very old.

"What kind of a gun is that?" Frank asked. He got up and went over to look. Sinan translated Frank's question, and the man brought some things out of his pocket to show them.

"Hey Julia, look at this!" Frank urged. "This is really interesting."

I finished tying my shoes and went over to look. The man with the scythe was still staring narrowly at me.

"What are they?" I asked, looking down at a pile of tiny brass objects the man held in his hand.

"They're percussion caps," answered Frank. "This is a muzzle-loading percussion cap rifle—the kind of gun they used in the Civil War."

The man put the caps away. Out of another pocket he produced two steel balls the size of large marbles. Frank didn't have to explain what they were. They appeared capable of producing quite a hole.

"What does he shoot with this thing?" I asked.

"Birds."

"Where was it made?" Frank asked. Sinan translated, and the peasant shrugged. He didn't know.

I'm sure he didn't care either. It was a powerful weapon, and with it he could blow a bird to smithereens. He lifted the gun to his shoulder, pointed it uphill, and took aim at a low, globular clump of thorns about twenty yards away.

CRASH! The rifle kicked into the man's right shoulder, and the clump of thorns disappeared in a cloud of dust. He brought the gun down and solemnly looked at us for approval. Everyone agreed that it had been a very impressive demonstration. He then showed us how the weapon was loaded, first the wadding, then the charge, more wadding, then the ball, and more wadding. After he had finished tamping it all down with the ramrod, the man and his companion said good-bye and set off again down the trail. They were talking and laughing loudly to each other in the rough, guttural tones that must have been Kurdish.

We hoisted the packs and set out on our way up the mountain. The trail soon lost itself among the rocks, giant smooth shapes that thrust their blackness out of the volcanic soil. As the trail wound among the rocks we sometimes lost sight of the summit overhead. Fifteen minutes up the trail we found several more fields where wheat had been grown. If anything, they were smaller than Kemal had described, mere patches of rocky earth tucked in among the rocks. The grain had been harvested, and only stubble remained.

It was past 4:30 when we left the fork. The late afternoon sun soon began to work its magic. The landscape became boldly etched in gold and shadow. We marched along the path at a slow, steady pace, breathing softly from the exertion. I looked at the view and ahead at my two companions. I was tired and aching, but I felt happy to be walking with them. Sinan looked gorgeous.

We came to the spring a little after six o'clock. It was just as the two peasants had described. A thick, knotted stake had been driven into the ground, and hidden up in the rocks to the right was a small place where water gushed out of a cleft in the stone and collected in a pool before rushing off downhill to disappear beneath a large boulder. We drank from it in long, icy gulps and splashed the water over our faces.

To the left of the spring, and twenty yards above it, we found a beautiful campsite, a broad open area whose well-beaten earth showed that it had been used by many others before us. I took off my pack and looked with satisfaction at the spot. The rock against which we set our gear blocked the view of Hasan Gazi, but before us the lake lay glistening in a landscape of golden mist. We were tired. The worst of the climb was over.

"This is wonderful!" Frank exclaimed as he gazed off into the valley. "Hey look! There's an eagle!" He pointed to a large bird floating far below us in the northwest.

Sinan grabbed his binoculars to take a look. He laughed gaily as he finally got the bird in focus.

"I am sorry, Frank," he said, "but it is not an eagle. It is a vulture."

Frank laughed along with Sinan and me.

"Well, you must admit," he said, "it looks very nice."

"You're right, Frank," I agreed. We stared a few seconds longer at the view. Late afternoon had become evening, and within an hour there would be no light. "We'd better make dinner while we can still see," I said.

We went back to where we had set the packs and started getting things organized. Sinan took the collapsible water bottle and went downhill to the spring, while Frank started laying out the groundsheets. I dug my little brass stove out of the pack and settled down to the task of getting it lit. To my delight it was no problem at all. The heat of the afternoon, combined with the change in altitude, must have built up the pressure inside, because when I opened the valve the gas spurted up immediately. The burner was soon roaring in the stillness of the mountainside, and in a few minutes I concocted a stew of potatoes, onion flakes, and some salt beef from the expedition larder. We wolfed it down along with *yufka* and white cheese, as well as Turkish powdered lemonade mixed in a canteen. Then we cleaned the dishes as the distant mountains faded into night. I was drying one of the pots with a bandanna when I heard something.

"Listen."

We froze. There was no wind. To the north, across the vast emptiness, the gray mountains lay cloaked in a light dusting of mist. It came again, the sound that I had heard, from above, below, from somewhere in the emptiness around us. A wailing, very distant and faint, like the sad, inscrutable songs I sometimes heard the workers sing at the castle.

"It is someone singing, I think," said Sinan. "Maybe a shepherd."

"Yes," I answered. But Kemal had said that there were no shepherds on this side of the mountain. We stood listening half a minute more but heard nothing.

An uneasiness settled upon us like the chill of fast-approaching night. As the land radiated its heat upward in the thin air we finished the dishes and set them aside for use in the morning. Then in the murky half-light we scattered into the rocks and left our contributions to the soil of Hasan Gazi.

When I came back to the campsite the two men had already unrolled their sleeping bags and were in the process of getting inside. I laid out my foam pad between the two of them and pulled the sleeping bag out of its sack. Then I took off my boots and slipped into the bag amid the loud squishing of nylon. After zipping myself in I stripped down and stuffed my clothes into the sleeping bag sack for use as a pillow. Then folding my arms behind me I lay back and savored my well-earned aches and pains.

It was dark by then, and the stars had emerged bright and sparkling in the clear air. We were expecting a full moon in an hour or so. Frank and Sinan were lying just like me, looking up at the stars. *Maybe tomorrow*, I thought.

Is it really so vulgar for me to admit that mountains turn me on? They do, Lord, how they do. I lay there and remembered all the times that Joe and I had grappled with each other on the ground in the middle of nowhere. There had been one especially delightful afternoon in the White Mountains. I barely managed to suppress a laugh at the memory of it. That had been about four thousand feet up. I wondered what it might be like at ten thousand. Thinner air, lighter heads, more gasping for breath. I laughed aloud.

"What are you laughing about, young lady?" Frank asked.

"Nothing," I said, "just thinking."

"Yeah," he breathed, "it's a good place to think all right. I know a lot of people who could use a place like this to get away to."

"The men you work with, you mean?"

He answered slowly, quietly. "Oh yes, the parolees of course. And the people in the office." He paused for a second. "But mostly I guess I was thinking about my son."

"Your son? What does he do?"

He laughed softly. "Do? I don't know exactly *what* he does. The last time I saw him was a year ago. Ran into him on the street in Detroit. He was wearing a fur coat and was getting out of a white Eldorado Cadillac. He had two girls with him. It was the first time I had seen him since my wife died three years before. He told me he was working as a music promoter."

"Really?"

"No, *not* really. That was a lie and I knew it. I'm not a parole officer for nothing. The guys I talked to didn't want to tell me much, but in the end I found out he's a dealer, one of the biggest in Detroit."

"No."

"Yes, a successful businessman at age twenty-five. Selling dope. I think he could use a place like this to get away and look at himself. What he'll probably get instead is the state prison."

I lay there for a moment and listened to my own breathing. Sinan had turned on his side to listen to us.

"I don't tell many people about my son," Frank went on, "but it seems like up here you could talk about anything and it wouldn't matter."

"I'm beginning to see now why you came to a place like this for a vacation."

"Yes," Frank said, chuckling softly, "I had a month of vacation saved up, and I made up my mind this year I was going to do something as completely different as possible from my other vacations. And I sure did. Turkey. Tanyeri. It's hard to believe we're on the same earth as Jackson, Michigan."

"I know." I looked up at the stars' white fire. Over eight thousand feet up on the side of a mountain in Kurdistan, it didn't seem possible that we were connected to anything else.

"Julia," Frank said abruptly, "you're a beautiful woman."

That startled me a bit. "Thank you, Frank," I managed to say.

"In fact," said Frank, "I like you so much that I worry about you."

"That's liking me too much."

"No, it isn't. Good night, Julia."

"Good night, Frank."

"Good night, Julia." I turned to look at Sinan.

"Good night," I said.

I drew the hood around my head and closed my eyes. But I couldn't sleep. I never can the first night out on a trip, and this first night was no exception. I tossed and turned for several hours, my mind besieged by memory and anticipation. When I finally dozed off the moon had risen over the northeast shoulder of the mountain.

Around midnight I woke and heard in the distance what I knew must have been the cry of wolves. I lifted my head instinctively to look but saw only black rock and a landscape flooded with moonlight. They howled again in the distance as I huddled in the sleeping bag and listened to the life flow through my veins. How had they managed to survive? After the forests, the lions, the other game? How had they done it? The mere knowledge that they had succeeded left me feeling peaceful and alone. *Bless them*, I whispered soundlessly to the rock beneath me, *Bless these Thy children in their hour of doom.*

The sun rose too early for our taste Thursday morning but mercifully waited behind the boulders of the northeast ridge. We finally bestirred ourselves around eight o'clock. I struggled into my clothes and got up slowly, stretching my aching muscles, grateful for the knowledge that today was going to be an easy day. I went down to the spring and splashed cold water on my face, then came back and set to work on the stove. It took about half the book of matches, but I finally got it going. The morning's breakfast delicacy was boiled bulgur with lots of sugar and raisins. It was edible.

By 9:30 we were back on the trail again. The day had begun clear, but by ten o'clock large cumulus clouds were floating over the mountain obscuring the summit for up to ten minutes at a time. This made me apprehensive. We had seen more than a few days in the previous three weeks when the mountain was totally obscured by cloud. I did not want that to happen Friday morning.

The morning's hike provided few surprises. We saw only one more of the tiny wheatfields, this one a minuscule patch that had been harvested, as Sinan pointed out, not by cutting the grain but by pulling it up by the roots. He said this method was especially damaging to the soil's fertility. It was easy to see why. I wondered that it had produced anything at all.

By eleven o'clock we had entered the maze of rocks that Kemal had described. The trail, which up to then had climbed diagonally up the face of the mountain, leveled off and advanced toward the east almost parallel with the slope's contours. It wound in and out among the boulders, and once we turned into a blind alley and had to retreat. Then the trail took a sharp turn uphill again and passed between two towering granite slabs with just ten feet of clearance between them. Ahead I could see only the sky, and I knew we were getting close. We climbed, panting, to the top of the slope and followed the trail as it meandered through an even narrower passage. At last we came around a rock and saw below us the secondary crater and, in its center, the tomb of Hasan Gazi.

We had come out of the rock maze and were standing on a ledge thirty feet above the crater looking east. Behind us the mountain sloped upward toward the summit, now hidden by cloud and the jumbled wall of rock.

We hiked down the narrow path leading into the crater. The crater itself, some fifty yards in diameter and filled in with dirt, was flat and open, and studded with smaller rock outcrops. In the middle of the open space stood a tiny roofless ruin of raw stone, joined together long ago with mortar and left to decay on the mountainside. The four walls seemed barely large enough to enclose a grave. Scattered around its shell were many of the building stones that had fallen away over the centuries, leaving the walls jagged and uneven.

"Look over here," said Frank. He was standing in front of

a sun-bleached rock three feet high by three feet across. It was the rock Kemal had told us about. The flat surface had been carved out to make a bowl six inches deep and a bit more than a foot in diameter. The rock was clean, with no signs of blood. Evidently the peasants had not come to the tomb for a sacrifice on Monday.

We set our packs down against the rock and walked into the tomb through an entrance on the east side. Like the shell of the tomb, the grave of Hasan Gazi was mostly rubble. A heap of stones lay in roughly the shape of a rectangle inside, and at the far end of the heap, against the back wall, stood a rough, battered stone inscribed with Arabic characters. Sinan climbed over the stones and squatted down to look at it.

"What does it say, Sinan?" Frank asked.

" *'Hasan Gazi, Allah için fatih. 462.'* It means 'Hasan Gazi, conqueror for God.' The 462 is the Muslim year. If this date is correct, he could not have been at the battle of Manzikert, as we have said. He died too soon."

"Who was he, then?" I asked.

"He was just a *gazi*," Sinan said. "In those days if you had a good horse, good sword, and good bow any man could be a *gazi*. If you liked war and liked plunder—and if you lived long enough—you were a *gazi*. This Hasan Gazi lived long enough."

"Look at this stuff!" Frank exclaimed. He was standing on the left by a niche in the wall. It had to be the niche Kemal had described. Sinan and I moved closer. Frank was pointing to what looked like ordinary trash, shoved into the cracks in the wall—bits of cloth, scraps of paper, and wads of human hair.

"What is it?" I asked.

"Offerings, charms," Sinan said. He pulled out one of the scraps of paper to show us. It was covered with Arabic scrawl.

Frank pulled out another scrap, which had more of the same.

"What does it say?" I asked.

"I can't read it. It's very badly written. Probably it is verses from the Koran."

The *gazi*'s tomb may have been rubble, but there were plenty of peasants who revered it nonetheless. Sinan and Frank walked out of the tomb, but I lingered a moment. If the *gazi* really had been a plunderer and bringer of destruction he certainly had received his just reward. Even the pathetic tokens of homage seemed an insult to his memory. A shadow had fallen across the crater as we stood talking, and standing there in the tomb, leaning on my ice axe, I was powerless to resist the chill that inched down my spine and gripped the flesh on my arms. In the sunlight the tomb was a fly-specked ruin, a heap of rock and debris. But shadowed by clouds at nine thousand feet, with snow lying in patches under the rocks, and a cool, sunless breeze blowing from the west, Hasan Gazi and his tomb became something quite different. There in that wilderness I suddenly thought of Joe's back turned toward me as he lay sleeping in the night. Of his ribs, his spine, the curve of his shoulder muscle. I saw the smoothness and the strength, like those lava boulders piled up against the sky. I felt again the ache of knowing that, like those boulders and that rubble, his back had been a wall, part of a thing I would always be separate from and could never hope to comprehend. I remember lying there at night whispering "I love you" and, again, "I love you," to his sleeping form. And moving closer, I would cower in the warmth of his flesh. But there was no shelter in the words, no shelter in the wall that lay there breathing and mute.

I walked out of the tomb and found the two men sitting in silence on the edge of the sacrificial rock.

"Man, this is a spooky place," Frank said quietly.

"Yes," I breathed. A massive cloud moved over the mountain like a gray, formless hand poised to descend and smother us.

"Let's go," I said.

"Don't you want to eat lunch here?" Sinan asked.

"No, we do *not* want to eat lunch here. We'll eat lunch when we've found a campsite."

We hoisted our packs again and set off. As we marched up and out of the crater the cloud rolled past the summit of Hasan Gazi. Slowly, seemingly inch by inch, the incredible dazzling crown of the mountain was revealed, beckoning. I looked back and saw that the tomb, which minutes before had seemed so menacing, had become once again a harmless heap of stones in the sunlight.

The path became steeper as we hiked up through the rocky maze and out into the more open slopes above the tomb. We had turned and were climbing straight up the northeast spine of the mountain, on the path that would take us to the top on the following day. Breathing hard in the thin air, I found myself leaning more and more on my ice axe. It was going to be a blessing to leave the packs behind the next morning. The patches of snow became more numerous as we ascended, though none yet intruded on our path through the rocks. The sunlight and the effort kept us sweating, but the breeze held a chilling edge.

Just before two in the afternoon we found our campsite for the night, a clear and level spot among the rocks at the edge of the mountain's permanent snowfield. At that height the summit appeared only a rounded hump of snow stretching up and up to the edge of nowhere. A large boulder blocked our view back down the mountain in the direction of the tomb. We set our packs against this rock, then knelt down in turn and drank deeply from the trickle of water issuing from a nearby snowbank. The water was a bit sandy, but it felt deliciously cold as it went down.

We got out the *yufka* and white cheese and tore into them with barbaric ferocity. I'm sure I wouldn't have cared if the *yufka* really had been newsprint.

After putting away the food we got out the groundsheets and sleeping bags and laid them out at the base of the rock with the heads positioned so that we would be facing up the mountain. Frank had brought a paperback and lay back to read it. I sat in the lee of the rock and doctored my feet with moleskin and water from the canteen. Sinan sat on my right basking in the sun. I could feel myself becoming warm and drowsy, but I fought against the temptation. I looked at Sinan, who was leaning against the rock with his eyes closed.

"Don't go to sleep, Sinan," I said quietly.

"What?" He looked up.

"I said don't go to sleep."

"Why not? You can sleep too." He gestured with his head toward Frank. I looked to my left and saw that he had placed the book over his eyes and was dozing contentedly. Sinan and I smiled at each other.

"Not now, though. I want to sleep well tonight."

"You can do both."

"No, I can't. I know what I'm like." I started putting my shoes and socks back on. "Let's go exploring."

"Exploring? Where do you want to go?" He didn't seem very enthusiastic.

"I don't know. Let's just start there," I pointed west, across the north face of the mountain, "then maybe down a bit, cut back east toward the tomb, and end up here."

"That sounds like much walking, Julia."

"Come on, Sinan, we can't just sleep all afternoon. It will help us get in shape. And if it is too far, we can always cut it short."

"All right. Do you want to tell Frank?"

"No, let him sleep. He'll know we're around somewhere."

I grabbed the ice axe and a sweater, which I tied around my waist. Sinan picked up his poplar staff and the canteen, and we set off across the north face, moving west and slightly down the slope. It was easy going for the most part, and we picked our way eagerly through the rocks. The north face of Hasan Gazi was concave, formed like a giant inverted amphitheater that narrowed toward the top. Looking up toward the middle of the north side I could see that near the top it became appreciably steeper than the ridge we would be climbing the next morning. Fifteen minutes' walk brought us to a barrier of rock at the edge of a narrow couloir, a snow-filled trough some twenty yards wide running from the permanent snowcap down the mountainside. It was one of the long ribbons of snow we had seen from the valley. The trough was walled in by rock all along its length, and across the band of snow halfway up the north face we caught a distant glimpse of the rockfall that impeded progress up that side.

"Shall we go on?" I asked.

"Why not?"

We climbed over the rocks and set out carefully across the soft snow of the couloir. At about the middle, standing up to my boot-tops in snow and looking down the steep trough, I suddenly got an idea. I turned to Sinan, who was behind me.

"I know! Instead of going straight on, let's slide down on this and cut back to the east side."

"Slide down?" He seemed startled for a moment, but then he smiled and said, "All right. Why not?"

"Of course! It's not as steep as it looks. The worst we'll get is wet pants. Look, just be sure to hold the pointed end of your staff ready so you can slow yourself down. Let's go!"

I sat down in the snow and pushed off. In a few seconds I was rocketing down the mountain on the seat of my pants.

"WHEEEEEeeeee!" we squealed, and the cries went echoing off into the rocks. Down, down, down we slid, slowing ourselves as we dug into the snow, then faster again, on and on.

"WHEEEEEEEEEEEeeeeeeeeee!"

"Julia, stop!" Sinan called out behind me. I jammed the pick of my ice axe into the snow and came to a halt. Sinan slid down level with me and got to his feet. He was laughing happily. We were both laughing.

"Julia!" he gasped, "you must stop! Remember we have to climb all the way back!"

"You're right," I granted, and I too got to my feet. My bottom was like a block of ice. We couldn't stop laughing. Walking over to the edge of the couloir, we climbed up and over the mass of jagged rock heaped alongside. Ahead of us was more rock, fallen long ago or pushed down by glaciation.

"Listen!"

I stopped in my tracks and tried to hear above the sound of my own panting. A murmur like water, low and elemental, came from somewhere nearby. We walked over to a large boulder and looked down into the crevices between the rocks piled under our feet. Deep in the cracks under the dark stones a secret torrent was drumming, and bending closer to look we heard the murmur swell to a roar as the black water gushed headlong and seething toward the valley.

"Beautiful," I breathed in awe. "It's wearing the mountain away. Where does it go?"

"To the Tigris. To Baghdad."

Still panting lightly, I knelt and listened to the water rushing beneath us. "Wonderful."

Sinan sat down in a small open space at the base of a granite monolith that blocked our view of the summit. I got up and joined him. I untied my sweater, rolled it up for a pillow, and lay back on the ground. The low voice of the water murmured in the back of my mind: *I miss you, I miss you.* The sun poured its warmth into our island among the rocks, and I closed my eyes, weakened by the power of it. Soon I knew I would either melt or disintegrate entirely as a personality. Was I expecting too much from this beautiful innocent? For he really did seem innocent, his blushes, bluff, and posturing masked an adolescent soul. No, it was a natural consequence of fresh air and warmth, this oceanic, earth-swallowing desire. The water breathed on: *I want you, I want you.* I glanced over at Sinan, now lying beside me on his back, his eyes closed against the glare and heat of the sun. Was he indifferent or merely enduring, with the grit and stoicism of his race? I looked up at the sky and felt an attack of insanity coming on.

"Sinan."

"Yes?" *What do I say?*

"Sinan . . . I feel very happy."

He smiled, opened his mouth to speak, then stopped as a fearful expectation in me said, *No, Sinan, I know it was a platitude, but please don't give me a platitude in return.*

A split second passed between us, like the moment when a thrown ball for one fleeting instant hangs weightless in the air at the top of its arc. And as the moment flashed by suddenly he was there, and it had begun. The murmur of the water gave way to laughter and breathing and we were naked, the clothes arranged beneath as best they could be. When Sinan rose above me he seemed to come out of the sun itself, towering against the sky in shadow, nailing my body to the earth with fire. Then, as he descended into my arms, the sun burst forth from behind his shoulder blinding me in shafts of piercing light. And the light became heat, became bright enveloping flesh as we raced, gasping, crying, laughing to the moist, sibilant delirium at the end.

Afterward we clung together, kissing and panting from

the effort. I laughed and laughed. It was delightful, this place, this mountain.

"Oh, Sinan, where did you learn to do that?"

"From a friend."

"Good for your friend." I laughed again.

"Why do you laugh?"

"I was thinking: if it's like this at nine thousand feet, what would it be like at the top?"

We laughed again and kissed, and I suddenly discovered that the ground was very hard beneath me. I stood and stretched my arms full length to the sky. I felt my fingertips tingling with warm blood and life.

"Sun, I love you!"

Sinan came from behind and held me, and I relaxed into his arms. Before us the mountain dropped away in a wilderness of rock, a gigantic amphitheater with only the two of us as spectators.

"You are so beautiful, Julia," he murmured in my ear.

"Yes, and you worry about me."

"I do, yes."

"Don't you have a girl friend, Sinan?"

"No."

"You should. You're very beautiful, too."

A breeze moved across the mountain, causing us to shiver. I broke free and reached down for my clothes. Sinan took my shoulder and I came back into his arms.

"No, Julia, not yet."

"But I'm cold."

"Again."

"The ground is very hard."

"Again." I felt him growing against me.

"No, tomorrow back at the castle."

"Again."

"All right." I smiled up at him. "But this time *you* get the rocks in your back."

He laughed at that. But in the end he agreed.

Ten minutes later I was putting on my rumpled clothing and laughing at Sinan, who was playing the martyr about his sore back. My watch said that it was after three o'clock.

"What shall we do with the rest of this glorious afternoon?" I asked, picking up my ice axe and waving it at the sky.

"I think we should go back to Frank."

"Why?"

"To see if he is okay."

"Of course he is. You just want to sleep, don't you Sinan?"

"Yes, all right, why not?" He grinned sheepishly.

"Because you'll sleep better tonight if you don't. Now, what shall we do with the rest of the afternoon?"

I thought of the fantasies that Joe and I sometimes used when we were camping. Children's games to set the heart pumping. I turned to Sinan.

"I know! I see myself . . . I see myself on a mountaintop in the mysterious East with a handsome sheikh who has kidnapped me for his harem. He is beautiful and brave, but I long for the cottage of my parents on the lakeshore. I have escaped from his camp while he lies down to sleep after lunch. But soon he discovers I am gone and takes off in pursuit through the rocks. My heart is full of terror as I flee down the mountain. My diaphanous veils catch on the jagged boulders, impeding my progress. What will he do when he catches me? His eyes are like fire and he is strong as an ox." Sinan listened to this with an embarrassed, incredulous smile.

"You are crazy," he said.

"Just give me two minutes' head start."

"All right. I will play your game. But be careful on the rocks!"

I ran off toward the east across the open expanse of the mountain's north face. I set a course calculated to bring me back to our summit path slightly above the *gazi*'s tomb. Glancing about at the expanse of rock and snow, I felt like an ant, exhilarated by my own insignificance. The going wasn't bad, but soon I was panting from the effort and excitement. Occasional patches of loose rock along the slope reminded me not to be too enthusiastic.

Pausing briefly, I looked ahead to the black rocks carpeting the northeast ridge. Another ten minutes at this pace would bring me back to the vicinity of the tomb. If I could keep up the pace. Looking back I saw that Sinan had set out after me. I could see him in the distance as he scrambled over a rock, canteen dangling and poplar staff working the ground.

I pressed on, climbing past another boulder and encountering a massive snowdrift ten yards across. Walking gingerly, I could hear the gurgle of water underneath, and looking to the left down its white sloping length, I could see the stream gushing out some fifty feet below. At the other side I looked back quickly for Sinan, but he had momentarily dropped from sight behind some rocks. Panting and giggling from the made-up adventure, I moved on toward the east.

Gradually the landscape was changing as I approached the northeast ridge. The loose, cindery gravel and open terrain gave way to the large igneous outcrops dominating that quarter of the mountain. Fifteen minutes after beginning the chase I had entered the maze of black rock. As the paths became more defined I picked up the pace. I cut left down through a narrow gap in the rock, then right again. Stopping for a moment, I looked up open-mouthed at the rocks hulking about me, hearing no sound but my own panting. The path wound through more of the maze and down again to the left. It continued downward, but I turned right at the first opening and headed east between the boulders. The ground rose slightly, then cut back up the mountain. At last, after several more twists and turns, I came out at the upper edge of the secondary crater, about fifty yards up the slope from where we had first seen the tomb earlier in the day. I was panting and sweating from the exertion, but as I stood there looking down at the tomb a cold breeze passed over my arms making me shudder. I untied the sweater from around my waist and put it on. By this time the clouds had backed off, and to the east the snow-dappled mountains stretched away limitless to the horizon.

"Juliaaaa. . . ." Sinan called, back somewhere beyond the rocks. I smiled and shivered again. My every nerve ending had come alive with the childish excitement of hide-and-go-seek, the breathless wait behind the door to scare the day-lights out of your best friend. I didn't answer.

The mountain was utterly silent. Down in the crater the bones of Hasan Gazi waited patiently for another millennium to pass. I turned from my view of the tomb to look for a hiding place in the rocks, and that's when I saw the man watching me.

Wearing the ragged clothes of a peasant, he stood about ten yards away in the shadow of a rock along the path I had just climbed. For perhaps five seconds we stared at each other before he walked out into the sunlight and gave me my first real look at his face. It was a vision of horror: his face did not exist. It was at though his image had been painted by a mad artist who had taken the heel of his hand to his canvas, smearing the features into oblivion before they had dried. It was a nonface, a mottled, pasty scab whose eyes, nostrils, and mouth appeared only as functional slits that had somehow survived the devastation. To complete the grotesque picture, the man's coarse black hair had been combed up and back in a horribly exaggerated pompadour.

I was stunned. I wanted to run or scream, but I couldn't. Shock gripped my arms like those long fingers of snow clutching the slopes above us. The man stood in the sunlight in the middle of the path, bent forward slightly, arms at his sides, talking in a hoarse, guttural monotone. He shuffled slowly toward me, talking all the while, and still the terror inside me could not break out and form itself into words. How many times before I had known this in dreams, the dark, silhouetted figure appearing in a doorway, poised just beyond my bedroom. But the *face*—the face was *nothing*. It was nothing in the darkness and in the light as it floated toward me in the depths of the nightmare.

"What—stop!" I raised the ice axe against the man in a crude and pathetically unthreatening gesture. I felt lost, frightened, and unutterably stupid. It was the time to be cool and heroic, and I was failing miserably. The man hesitated when he saw the ice axe, his blank, melted face registering no expression at all.

"Julia!" Sinan came in sight on the path behind the man and stopped when he saw us. His face registered surprise, then went slack with horror as the man turned to face him. For an instant they looked at each other. Then the man was gone, darting into the rocks from which he had appeared.

"Julia! What—" I relaxed my pose with the ice axe and let it fall. Sinan started into the rocks after the man.

"Stop, Sinan, let him go!"

I sat down on the ground and let the aftershock roll through my body. Sinan hurried over beside me.

"Are you all right?" I nodded yes. I was not all right. I was frightened silly and humiliated.

"What was he doing?"

"Nothing—I don't know."

"Was he trying to touch you?"

"Yes—no, I don't know really. He just kept on talking. He looked awful."

"Yes." We sat and thought about that terrifying face.

"Who was he, Sinan? Have you seen him before?"

"No. I have never seen him in the villages."

"Do you suppose he lives up here?"

"I don't know. Maybe he only came up to the tomb."

"Do you think he might have been watching us back there?"

"Maybe. I don't know. But how did he get this far over without being seen? We could have seen him in that open area."

"Yes, but we weren't really looking for him. And he must know these rocks very well. What an awful face."

"Yes, I have never seen anything like it. Maybe that is why he is up here."

"What do you mean?"

"Maybe he came to the tomb to pray. To ask for help. They do that, you know. Or maybe he lives up here."

"How?"

Sinan shrugged. "Maybe it is a sickness that has made his face like that. Maybe he was sent out of the village."

"Maybe he's a leper."

"Yes. Who knows? Or, of course, fire. Many babies are burned every year in these villages. They fall into the ovens that heat the houses."

I considered this for a moment. The more I thought the stupider I felt. Now that the man was gone I could feel sympathy for him: an outcast, probably, carrying that face with him for the rest of his life. He hadn't really threatened me. But he was horrifying. And he was probably back in the rocks now, watching us. I grabbed my ice axe and stood up.

"Let's get out of here," I said.

"Yes, you are right." We looked at each other, and I saw the same unease in his eyes. We turned our backs on the tomb and started climbing.

Half an hour later we arrived, exhausted and sweating, at the campsite. Frank was leaning back against the rock reading, his gold-rimmed spectacles propped on the end of his nose.

"Hello there, you two. You've been gone a long time."

"What time is it?"

"Past 4:30. What have you two been doing to keep yourselves amused?"

I smiled in spite of my weariness.

"We've been exploring, Frank."

"Yes, Frank," Sinan said, "Julia has found a friend."

"Yes. We're not alone up here."

"Really?" Frank put his book down and looked up at us over the rim of his spectacles. "What do you mean?"

I told him the story, leaving out our little dalliance by the rock. Frank listened in silence.

"Well, do you think this guy's dangerous?" Frank asked. Sinan and I looked at each other.

"No, he is very ugly but not dangerous."

"I agree," I said, "but I certainly hope we won't see him again."

"Do you think there's any danger that he'll steal our stuff tomorrow?"

"Maybe," Sinan replied, "but I don't think so. Usually these peasants are quite honest. And our sleeping bags belong to the gendarmes. If they were stolen there would be trouble."

"Why do you think he's up here?" Frank asked.

We told him what we had discussed below. "Hell, in that case," he said, "I don't think it's anything at all to worry about. Some poor guy living up here alone, probably. Kemal told us we would see people."

"You might think differently if you'd seen his face," I said.

"Never mind, Julia," Frank said almost jovially, "let's forget about it." He put down his book and stood up. "And I have a surprise. Something to help us forget." Walking quickly to the snowbank where we got our water, Frank reached back behind a rock for something hidden from our view. Then with a grand flourish and a shower of white he pulled forth a large dark bottle with ice and snow still clinging to it. He stood there proudly, his face wreathed in an excited smile, like a father playing Santa Claus on Christmas morning.

"What is it?" I asked, dumbfounded.

"Champagne!" Frank answered. "Turkish champagne."

"But where did you get it?"

"I carried it up here. In my pack. I kept it hidden. I wanted to surprise you."

"Frank, you're a saint!" I said. "That must weigh a ton."

"Well, I thought if I was going to haul champagne up here I might as well do it right. I got it from Kemal, out of his own private stock. It's him you really have to thank."

"Frank, you are wonderful," Sinan said.

"Well, let's open it!"

So while Frank brought out his pocket knife to peel away the foil wrapping, I got together our deluxe service of plastic cups. The cork came out with a delicious, resounding pop, and as the champagne sparkled in the sunlight we toasted Kemal and Frank. We sat on a rock on the east side of camp where we were in the sun and could see the view. I took off my shoes and suddenly felt very free.

"How do you like it?" Frank asked us.

"Excellent."

"Very good."

"I agree," said Frank, "and the amazing thing is, it's only about two dollars a bottle."

"At this altitude it's priceless," I observed. I was a bit giggly, not from the alcohol but from the exhilaration of drinking champagne at that altitude. I had another sip. It really was very good. Getting to sleep was going to be no problem at all. With the warm sun of late afternoon and the companionship of friends I felt much better about everything. The wine had blotted out the memory of our "Quasimodo" in the rocks and in its stead I saw Sinan's dark body looming above me in an indelible image. It had been a full day: love on the mountainside, horror at the tomb, warm sun and cold champagne at ten thousand feet. A day to remember. The next day would seem almost anticlimactic: a few hours' ascent, then back to Tanyeri and the castle. And on Monday the trip to Tatvan to get the train away from this mass of snow and rock that had kept me fascinated for so long. Sitting on the rock, I held up my clear plastic cup and looked at the world through a prism of champagne.

"Julia, what do you see in that glass of wine anyway? I don't think we should have given you this stuff."

"Quiet, Frank," I said smiling at him. "Can't you see anything in those bubbles? Look again." I leaned back on the flat surface of the rock and looked through the champagne. Before us the jumble of mountains lay cloaked in a light mist. The golden champagne sparkled in the glass, its threads of tiny bubbles waving sinuously as the liquid rocked gently from side to side.

Frank was looking through his glass with an amused smile. He brought it to his mouth and took a healthy sip. "Yeah," he breathed with satisfaction, "this is what serious drinking is all about." He patted his belly and took another sip. "I really feel mellow. If only I didn't have to walk any more everything would be perfect."

"Your feet pretty bad?" I asked. He was wearing sandals at the time.

"Only when I walk on them. Actually they're getting better every second."

"Good. Keep on drinking."

"I will, Julia dear, I will." He picked up the bottle and refilled our cups.

"How are your feet, Sinan?" Frank asked.

"Good enough," he said noncommittally.

"And bad enough too, I'll bet." I couldn't resist it.

He smiled grudgingly at me and nodded his head. "Yes, I will admit it. They could be better."

"Well never mind. Mine are pretty bad too."

"I think we ought to call it off tomorrow," Frank said. "Just stay here and loaf."

"Then what?"

"Well, I'm sure we can talk Sinan into running down to the 7–11 for some more champagne. You wouldn't mind that, would you Sinan?" Sinan just laughed. "Then we can sit here all day and watch bubbles."

"Good idea. What will we eat?"

"Eat? Snow, I guess."

"Snow?"

"Yeah, snow. It's high in protein crystals. And it's completely free of cholesterol. And it'll keep the champagne cold." He topped up our glasses again. I took another gulp.

We sat and gazed at the bubbles some more. I was feeling very tipsy. Back and forth the bubbles wove in the sunlight, beckoning, beckoning. . . .

"My bubbles," announced Sinan, "are like a beautiful *danseuse* in a *gazino* in Istanbul. She is trying to seduce me. She has covered her belly with honey and she wants me to lick it clean."

"Why, Sinan!" I exclaimed, "you're full of surprises today! I never knew you had such an imagination."

He laughed shyly. "I guess it is my 'romantic Turkish

soul,' " he said, carefully enclosing the phrase in verbal quotation marks.

"I never knew Turks had romantic souls," said Frank. "You seem like the most straightforward, matter-of-fact people I've ever known."

"Yes, but that is just one side. And, of course, we always do our duty like soldiers. But what do you think the men do when they sit in the *çayhane* and drink tea and listen to music? They are dreaming."

"That's certainly true," Frank said.

"But also I think we dream because the situation with women is so bad. They are shut away all the time—even in the big cities—and so we dream. Of course, in the villages also. The women stay at home and work in the fields. The men stay in the *çayhane* and they dream. They are bored."

"But it's their own fault, isn't it?" I said. "They're the ones who shut the women away."

Sinan gave a shrug of bewilderment. "I know, I know. But it is their nature. It is what you call a vicious cycle."

I laughed a rather cynical laugh and sipped my wine. Some vicious cycle, all right. Women shut away to work and to breed. Result: too many children. Result: crowding, overpopulation. Result: few jobs to go around, unemployment. Result: men sit idle in the teahouses and dream. About what? Women and jobs. About the women and jobs their own dreams and customs deny them. Ah, the insights of alcohol. *In vino veritas.* I laughed again. I was feeling so good I didn't even care. Frank filled up the glasses to the brim. It was the last of the champagne.

"Cheers everybody," I said.

"Serefe."

"Down the hatch."

The bottle had gone very fast. The sun had settled toward the horizon on our left, and it sat poised on the mountain's west shoulder. In another half hour it would sink behind the curtain of rock and leave our camp in shadow.

"Shall we start thinking about supper?" I asked.

"Sure, let's think about supper. But for Jesus' sake, let's not do anything about it. It's too early. Let's finish the champagne first. Right, Sinan?"

"Right, Frank."

"What are we having tonight, Julia?" Frank asked.

I laughed. "Well, Your Highness, I thought we could mix a lot of junk together in a pot. Boil the bulgur, throw in the salt beef, then add the two packages of freeze-dried chicken with rice that I brought. How does that sound?"

"Beautiful."

"*Fevkalade.*"

We sat there on the rock for another five minutes and finished the wine. Then I put my shoes on and started getting things together for dinner. The three of us floated about the campsite fetching water, giggling, digging out pots. Luckily we had the big flat rock to use as a table. In my state I'm sure I couldn't have managed cooking on the ground. As it was, the stove proved all but unmanageable, and in the end I had to prime it with a healthy squirt of white gas. A risky business, but it worked. The water took forever to boil. We threw together the hash, complete with the chicken resuscitated like the phoenix from its freeze-dried ashes. Reviews were mixed, but no one denied it had substance. Plenty of substance.

And then there was dishwashing, for me always the worst part of camping. But luckily it was Sinan's turn. And did he hate it! We stood around and laughed our heads off at his martyrdom. I'm sure he had never before washed dishes in his life. In the end Sinan didn't get them very clean anyway, so as he watched in amazement I grabbed some sand-cum-dirt from near the snowdrift and proceeded to scour our pot and plates with it. When they were all thoroughly plastered with the grainy muck I held them out very daintily by the fingertips as Frank rinsed them with hot water from the big pot.

That done we shut off the stove at last, and silence returned to the mountainside. The cooking, eating, and washing had taken us past seven o'clock, and the setting sun cast its last patches of golden light upon the distant peaks. I packed away the pots and the stove for good. We were through with them, having decided to strike out for the summit as soon as possible in the morning without a hot breakfast. I wanted to get there and be done with it, no more cooking, no more dishwashing. I carefully wrapped the stove in its plastic bag, then put it inside the two pots, stacked one inside the other. The plates, nested all together with the utensils inside, went into another plastic bag that I put into the top compartment of the pack along with the food. I brought out the *yufka*, the white cheese, and the chocolate for use the next day.

Frank and Sinan had gone into the rocks on the west to relieve themselves, so I walked over to the east side of camp to look at the view. I sat down on the rock and listened. Every cell of me strained forward to touch the chill and darkness settling over the land. I held my breath and looked off into the abyss. A lonely cloud wandered over a peak, a bird floated aloft in the stillness. The blue-gray, lightly misted mountains, great raw, jagged files of them, stretched to the horizon. And in the emptiness a voice again, the same as the night before but clearer, more compelling. A melody of simple, timeless pain.

"Do you hear it?" Sinan asked. He had come back and was standing beside me looking down toward the tomb.

"Yes, I hear it," I murmured. "Now we know who was singing last night."

"Yes."

It seemed to be coming from the direction of the tomb, but I couldn't be sure. It could have come from anywhere. How surprised I was at the hollowness the man's voice awakened in me now that I couldn't see him or his face. A lonely song indeed. So distant I could barely hear it, floating off into that dark shroud now gathering round the mountains, quintessence of wolf-wildness, solitude, and rejection. *I feel for you now*, I thought, *but I hope I never see you again.*

The three of us stood listening as the darkness closed in. I wanted Friday to come with its swift, sure advance to the top, its dazzling view, and its quick return to the sureties of Tanyeri. For the first time since we started up the mountain I wondered if I really wanted to be there. It wasn't fear. There was nothing to be afraid of. It was the feeling that had come over me at the tomb, that of being an intruder in a place I could never really touch. I closed my eyes and sucked in my breath. With that breath I expelled my thoughts, pushing them out and away.

I opened my eyes. The land was nearly dark. Frank and Sinan were putting things away, getting their sleeping gear in order. I set out my small summit pack for use in the morning and made a trip of my own into the rocks. Minutes later, secure in our sleeping bags under the stars, we talked over plans for the next day: up at dawn, the summit by midmorning, explore the crater until noon, then back down to get the gear and return to Tanyeri. Gradually the talk died out as the realities of physical exhaustion and alcoholic torpor settled into our bodies. I lay between the two men gazing up at the emerging stars. Turning to the right I saw Sinan in his sleeping bag looking into my eyes. His face was dark, questioning.

"Good night," he murmured.

I reached out and caressed his cheek with my hand.

"Pretty dear," I whispered and settled into blank, exhausted rest.

There was light outside my cocoon of nylon and down, and I awoke to seek it out. Unzipping the bag several inches, I sat up and looked off to the east. Large masses of clouds hung level with our camp in the half-light. Somewhere in the east, beyond the mountains of Azerbaijan, the sun was gathering itself, preparing for day.

It was very cold. I fished my clothes out of the foot of the sleeping bag and put them on with impatient, jerking movements. On either side of me Frank and Sinan lay dark and motionless in their mummy bags. I decided to let them sleep a bit longer. I wanted to enjoy the sunrise alone. Unzipping the bag all the way, I slipped out of it and with trembling fingers began putting on my hiking boots. After finishing with the laces I stood up and pulled the down jacket from its stuff sack. The nylon came out crinkled and squashed, but slipping it on quickly I shivered with satisfaction as the down surrounded my arms with warmth. Thrusting my hands into the pockets I walked over to the flat rock on the east side of camp and sat down to watch the sun come up. The perlon rope lay coiled on top of my pack, and I put it under me as partial insulation against the rock's frigid surface.

Through a gap in the clouds I could see, at least temporarily, the dimly outlined ranges beyond which the sun would soon appear. Reaching into the top compartment of my pack I pulled out the canteen and took a long drink. I wondered how long the clouds would stand away from the mountain. There seemed to be many more than we had seen before. Looking down the mountain to the left, I saw the area of black rock that hid the *gazi*'s tomb now about to be engulfed by a large cumulus cloud. Prospects did not look good for a clear view from the top.

I started to look toward the east, but something had moved in that gray wilderness of rock. I turned my eyes back toward the tomb to find it. The cloud was closing in, and in the predawn grayness I strained forward trying to penetrate the mist. Nothing.

Jumping down from the rock I slung the perlon rope across my shoulders and chest bandolier fashion, walked downhill from our camp, and hopped up on another boulder to get a better view. Off in the east the sky had brightened, but the clouds were closing in fast. I stood on the rock for nearly a minute looking northeast down the slope toward the black rocks. Still I could see nothing.

Then in the distance a tiny, almost invisible figure appeared out of the mist and hung there, unmoving in the gloom. Then there was another figure. And another. And yet a fourth, darting from rock to rock up the mountainside. I stared at them for some seconds, reaching ever deeper into my lungs for breath. They were maybe half a mile away, running toward us. *Running.* There was no doubt of it. I turned and ran the few yards back up to our campsite. Both men were still.

"Sinan! Frank! Someone's coming!"

There was no response from either of them. Frank's dark, slumbering features lay framed by the lighter khaki hood of his sleeping bag. I moved past him to Sinan, who was turned away from me with his face nestled against and half hidden by a small pile of his own clothing.

"Sinan! Wake up!" I whispered kneeling behind him. I grabbed his shoulder and shook hard. I pulled him sharply toward me, and as his slack body rolled over in response to my efforts I looked down into eyes that were protuberant, staring, and immutably dead. The dark, linear bruises on his neck told why the mouth hung open as it did, waiting for breath that would never come again.

I staggered to my feet, fighting frantically for the air with which to make a sound. I could only gasp in dry, gagging horror.

"Frank!" I rasped in desperation. He didn't move.

"FRANK!" Almost a scream this time. No answer but a distant cry from down the mountainside.

I ran to the other side of the rock and looked down. The four men were still coming, but they were closer now, and I could see rifles slung on their backs. They were running. *Running. What kind of man can run up a mountainside at this altitude?*

I scrambled frantically back up to camp and ran to my pack leaning against the rock on the east side. Grabbing the ice axe, I stopped to look back in panting disbelief at the bodies of my companions lying strangled in the dirt. My eyes focused on the unruffled blue nylon of my own sleeping bag lying between Frank and Sinan, and at last I screamed, a low, full-throated cry of hatred and terror. The rocks, the snow, and Sinan's staring eyes coalesced in a vision of horror as through my nostrils, across my dry tongue swollen in fright, flowed the rancid taste of death.

I whirled and started up the mountain with the ice axe, but again I hesitated, breathless, as rationality cut through my panic for an instant. Looking down at my pack and seeing the instep crampons strapped to the side, I knew I would never get away without them. In a frenzy of indecision I looked down and saw the four men coming after me, now only minutes away. With a cry of impatience and terror, I virtually ripped the crampons from their holders and, fumbling frantically, my fingers shaking with the task, strapped each one to my feet. Then grabbing the ice axe, and with the rope still slung around me, I scrambled up through the rocks and onto the hard-crusted snow stretching away to the blue sky and nothingness.

Behind me as I hit the snow the silence was swept away by the sound of boots scurrying over rock and the hooting cries of men at the hunt. I tried to run faster and almost immediately fell on the hard snow. Getting to my feet, I glanced back for a second and saw a huge man in black boots coming up after me through the rocks. Frantically, I struggled on up the slope, the crampons digging well into the crust. A glimmer of sunlight shone from the east, and the sight of my own huge shadow stretching out ahead sent a shudder through me. Behind me more hoots and yells and then laughter as I heard the whump of a man falling in the snow. I fought the urge to look back. The loud crack of a rifle exploded across the mountain as a snowbank to my right sucked in the projectile with a short hiss and a brief, sparkling shower of crystals. More laughter from below. I ran on, frantically exhaling the thin air with loud, gasping sobs.

Gradually I realized to my horror that I was perceiving more than the sound of my own breathing, more than the crunch of my own boots against the snow. I knew without looking back that behind me the man was gaining, no matter how fast I tried to climb. Wearing leather boots on hard snow and after running all that distance, the monster was *still* gaining on me! I let out a cry of rage and frustration. I could move no faster, and still the man kept on coming, his gasps rising to a crescendo in my ears. Then, looking down in the snow, I saw the top of his shadow flicker briefly around the ankles of my own, and I sobbed again in frustration. I thought, *do something*, but what? His shadow had climbed halfway up my own. Suddenly the image surged forward and a disembodied hand snaked out to grasp my right boot.

I almost fell, but the hand slipped free and lay still for an instant in the snow. Seizing that instant, I brought my upraised foot down full force into the man's outstretched palm. The points went in deep, and as I wrenched my boot free I could see the four dark spots where his flesh had been torn open. The man, stretched out full-length on the slope from his lunge after me, shouted from the pain and reached out with the left hand to clasp his right wrist. In that moment, with two quick movements of my right foot, I kicked snow in his eyes and swung the sole of my hiking boot hard into the middle of his face. He screamed, and this time I didn't stay to look at the damage.

A bellow of rage exploded behind me, the crunch of boots on snow and then a low whump as the man slipped and fell on the slope. Again, in the distance, his partners hooted and laughed. As I left them behind I could hear loud, angry curses from my pursuer, and for a while there were more steps and crunches as he tried to catch me in his leather boots. But as I climbed higher and higher in the snow toward safety, the most memorable sound, boring deep into my skull and filling it with hatred, was the sound of far-off inscrutable laughter.

Some time later, over an hour, I thought, I allowed my legs to give way and sank back into the snow to rest. I had come up over the shoulder of the mountain that had blocked our view from the campsite, and the summit reared awesome above me, no more than an hour or two away. From the height of the sun, now beginning to melt the snowy crust, it seemed to be about eight o'clock. I had left my watch somewhere back at camp, so I had no idea of the exact time. But that didn't matter anymore. In fact, nothing seemed to matter anymore. I sat for several minutes hunched in the snow listening to the sound of my own panting. The wet soon penetrated my jeans, but I didn't move.

I clenched my teeth and tried to deal with the horror of the last few hours. I saw Sinan's face gagging in death, and I looked away. I saw Frank asleep and my own empty bag lying between them. *Why?* They could surely sell the gear for something. But *why?* And I remembered the laughter. There it was: for the laughter, the joke. And suddenly the whole thing seemed almost a culmination: the snake down the blouse, the water splashed in the face at the swimming pool, the quick feel on the subway, the man in the poplar grove and now this, the woman left behind to enjoy the joke and get hers in the morning. I remembered poor Sinan and Frank, and I wept with hatred. Below me, the now-solid mass of cloud had swallowed up the campsite completely.

But after all the hatred had been released I still had to decide what to do. It all depended on the men below, hidden by the thick curtain of cloud flowing down upon us from the north. Would they take the goods and flee, or continue their pursuit? For the time being, I felt safe enough where I was. I could perhaps stay hidden and sneak back down at night. I dismissed that idea immediately. Down those slopes again at night? Past the bodies of Sinan and Frank, through the rock maze and . . . *the freak at the tomb. Oh God.* I had forgotten about him. Had he been among the four? I had only briefly seen the face of the giant who pursued me. *He must have been among them,* I thought. He was the only one who could have known the location of our campsite. Or was he? We had seen the other two men lower down, the man with the rifle and his ever-staring companion. They must have known the route we had taken. And Sinan had said, *They know everything, these people.* It could have been anyone. I would not descend the northeast ridge. Never again.

I thought about going around to the south side, but that made no sense. It was unknown territory. Even if villages existed on that side, I might not find help. The murderers themselves might even have come from the south. And there would be the problem of getting back around to the north side, where I had to go.

There was simply no choice, I had to get to the west side. Kemal had said, *That's where the people are, that's where they graze the sheep in summer.* I had to get over there. But how? Straight across the north face. But the north face wasn't straight, it was concave. It curved in toward the center and became significantly steeper. I had seen it on the map. In the end it might take almost as much time as a trip over the top and down. And a path across the north face had two big disadvantages: it was still low on the mountain, and it was exposed. Below me, the men were hidden, but just as importantly I was hidden from them. The higher I went, the less visible I became. If I stayed at this altitude and followed the contours across the north face, the clouds might very well hold solid and screen me from them. But if the men looked up and happened to see me outlined against the snow, I would be trapped with the summit rampart above me and nowhere to flee. In the end there was only one option: up and over to the west side. With a sigh and a curse, I got to my feet and started walking.

I arrived at the summit around midmorning. I had stopped halfway up to take off my crampons and to tie the bandanna low over my eyes as a partially effective shield against the glare. It had helped only a little. When I reached the top I was exhausted and breathing heavily in air thinner than any I had ever breathed.

The summit of Hasan Gazi was a large open area dominated by a massive oval crater approximately one hundred yards long and fifty yards wide. The snow-covered sides of the crater sloped steeply toward its center, which was filled with snow to within about thirty feet of the rim. On my right, stretching along the northern rim of the mountain, was the low ridge of black rock that we had identified as the summit rampart, the highest point.

I wanted to get to the top, but first I had to find water.

138

Like my sunglasses and watch, the canteen had been left behind. I had tried eating snow, but it only made me sick. After four hours' march through that desert of snow I needed water badly. I searched around the rim of the crater and finally located a tiny trickle about halfway down the inside of the crater on the north side, where the sun shone most powerfully against the steep slope. The talus surface glistened from the melted ice, which dripped down to form a pool barely large enough to float a flower petal. Putting down the ice axe I knelt on the wet slope and sucked the puddle dry in a second. The water contained tiny particles of gravel, but it tasted cold and thrilling. I picked the gravel from my teeth and waited as the water trickled down and filled the cavity again. Placing my lips to the earth I sucked it dry. I did this again and again, for what must have been at least five minutes.

When I had finished, I climbed out of the crater and went up onto the rampart of rock that snaked along the north edge of the summit, extending down the east and west sides. It was easy to reach from the crater side and relatively level along the top. I stood on a rock and looked around.

The clouds blanketed all but a few of the peaks. Directly to the north, the massive hump of Süphan Dagh pushed through the clouds on the north shore of Lake Van. To the right, but much farther away in the northeast, I could see Ararat's tiny white cone. In the east and south, jagged snowy ridges appeared along the borders of Iran and Iraq.

I made my way over the rocks to the edge of the rampart. It wrapped around that side like a long rock wall. Immediately before me, the rocks fell away vertically to a vast, white amphitheater that sloped steeply to the masses of rock and cloud far below. The drop from the edge to the snowfield beneath could not have been more than a hundred feet at most, but from where I stood it seemed like infinity. I laid the rope on a rock and sat down, quivering with vertigo. A cold breeze stirred on the mountain. The clouds seemed close enough to touch: gigantic fluffs of down on which I longed to lie and sleep forever. Their dazzling white tops contrasted sharply with the gray beneath and made it nearly impossible for me to see anything through the trailing mist and shadows. I pulled the rolled bandanna lower over my eyes and stared into the narrow gaps in the cloud cover. I saw nothing but snow and rock and mist. The clouds floated lazily on, meshing, constantly veiling and revealing new parts of the mountain. I had always thought a fortune-teller's crystal ball would be like this: a shadowy, private dream world that told its secrets only to those who stared into it long enough. I could see nothing.

I woke from my reverie and remembered that I had to go on to the west side. In my exhausted trance I could have stayed there forever looking off into the clouds. At that height nothing seemed real. But I was in danger, and I had to get moving.

Slinging the rope over my shoulder, I picked up my ice axe and prepared to head west along the ridge. I looked off at Süphan Dagh and down once again at the ever-changing carpet of vapor before me. Through a gray, wispy opening in the cloud cover somewhere to the left and in the uncertain distance among the rocks, I saw something that yanked me out of my stupor and put me on the alert again. I crept to the edge of the cliff and knelt down. Breathing deeply, I stared into the grayness trying to pick up whatever it was that my brain had discerned. It moved again, far below and to the left, a tiny, black speck, almost invisible and occasionally hidden by the rock, moving toward the northwest ridge. I stopped breathing, paralyzed by what I saw. Then there was another dark figure evanescently silhouetted against a patch of snow. Two of them. I looked on, mesmerized, hoping against hope that I would see four figures instead of two. I did not. There were only two. I put my hands over my face and hid my eyes from the sun shooting its glare into me. The unthinkable had happened: they must have split up in two groups, one for the west, the other for the east. They were in the game to stay.

I got back to my feet and backed away from the edge of the cliff. Once again I considered going down the south side. It was tempting, to be sure. But when I tried to get back around the killers might be in an even better position than they were now. No, somehow I had to go down the middle of the north face. That was obviously the place they least expected me to go. If I could make it down into the clouds I might have a chance. Lost in the mist in the middle of that huge expanse they would never find me. But how would I get down? Not over the cliff. I had learned how to rappel one terrifying afternoon at summer camp in New Hampshire eighteen summers before, but I had no desire to repeat the experience. I flinched at the memory of it: the fearless, bullying face of the instructor, the mixed group of campers silent with their own fears but still managing wordlessly to coerce me over the edge. I remembered rigging the rope—that was easy enough—and then the drop backward, my boots jarring against the rock, my heart frantic with a fear that kept me from doing anything correctly. I had done it two or three times more, but I hated it all the same. No, I had to find some other way, and the only other way was to make an end run around the rampart on the east side, cutting back in toward the middle, and then down.

Picking up the ice axe, I made my way back over the rocks and down onto the snow-covered ground by the crater's edge. I hurried east past the crater and started descending the ridge

I had just come up. To my left, the summit rampart jutted out to the east and then down the mountain, both sides at that point presenting a sheer rock wall that prevented anyone from passing. Only some two hundred yards down the slope did the barrier end, descending into the snow in a series of jagged spires. I had to pass around these before cutting back to the middle. Unfortunately, I didn't get very far.

As I trundled along heel first in the snow, I looked down and saw the end to my fool's paradise. Far off on the north-east ridge but well out of the clouds, two more dark figures were silhouetted against the snow. And they were moving. I hunched down in the snow, hoping that they hadn't seen me. It didn't seem so. The men trudged along at a steady, unbroken pace, one of them using what appeared to be a rifle for a walking staff. They seemed to be only about fifteen minutes from the summit. So there went my easy end run around the rocks. I got back to my feet and fled headlong back up the slope.

I clambered up onto the ridge again and ran west along the edge, trying to get as far out of sight as possible. The sun had reached its maximum power, and the glare from the clouds and snow and sky surrounded me in what seemed a halo of unreality. I stopped and looked about at the immensity of it all: the clouds, the rampart, the vertical drop to the snow, and I felt like an insect about to be crushed by the boot of some anonymous, savage giant. My head throbbed and again I was thirsty, but I knew it was impossible to go back to the water now. I was at the edge of the cliff, and I had to go down.

I had to find a rappel point, and luckily there was no lack of them. Without looking very far I could see several good places to loop the rope. But I also wanted to find the place with the shortest drop to the snow. One hundred and twenty feet of rope when doubled for rappeling made only sixty feet, and the drop might easily be more than that. I searched desperately for the right spot, but panic blurred my perception and decisiveness. They all looked the same.

Gazing over the edge at the sheer drop, it didn't seem possible that I could descend it. I looked off to the right and saw that I was screened by the curving wall of rock and snow from the men advancing up that side. On the left there was no sign of anything. I looked down again and felt the rocks like silent, coercive spectators waiting for me to do what I had to do.

At last I chose a rock around which to loop the rope. It was rounded and squat and about the size of a large fire hydrant. I uncoiled the rope and flung one end of it over the cliff. Carefully holding the remaining end, I kneeled to look over the precipice and saw the red tangle of rope fallen in the snow beneath. There was certainly plenty of rope if I used it as a single strand. Passing the remaining end around my waist I dropped it down and pulled up the fallen rope so that the two ends were dangling together, about even. I looked down trying to judge the distance: they seemed to be just short of the snow, but close enough.

Standing up once again, I took the loop from my waist and slung it over the rock I had chosen. The doubled rope now hung down over the cliff. Fighting against the temptation to run back over the rocks and look for the two killers, I paused at the edge and tried to remember how it had been done at camp. I straddled the rope and took it around my left hip, then up and across my chest to the right side and down in back. I paused again. Was it right? I wasn't even sure of my own name. I picked up the ice axe and hung it over my left wrist by the strap, using that hand to hold the rope in front of me. My right hand grasped the double rope in back, which, if I handled it right, would control my rate of descent. Thus rigged and swallowing hard, I backed up to the edge of the cliff and very gingerly started to walk down.

The rope dug hard into my pelvis as I descended, and I fought against the urge to hurry. I concentrated on keeping my right hand tight around the rope in back, momentarily expecting that it would simply give way and plunge me to my death. I was far too frightened to look down so I concentrated on the lug soles of my hiking boots as they scraped and jarred against the cliff face. Thus I inched down the cliff face, whimpering and cringing like the acrophobic coward that I am.

About halfway down I looked back to see how much rope was left. As I looked the mountain opened beneath me with dizzying, awesome depth, and the steeply sloping snowfield seemed to drop away into a gray, smoldering hell. My right shoe scraped and pawed at the rock wall, and I gripped the red-sheathed rope, clinging to it convulsively as though it were an electric wire. *Go down, stupid*, I cursed at myself, *don't hang there like an idiot.* I started again, inching down the cliff, wasting my strength with fear.

At last I came to the end of the doubled rope, but I was still about ten feet above the snow. I had to jump for it and pray that the snow was deep and soft. Not wanting to impale myself on the end of my ice axe I decided to drop it first. I let go of the upper rope and worked the strap of the axe off my left wrist. I held the axe before me for a second and looked at the distorted image of myself reflected along the chrome steel of the pick: bandanna low over the eyes, hair loose and blowing, lips cracked and open. I flung the ice axe spinning and flashing in a wide arc that ended with an easy thud in the snow.

Immediately after that sound there came another, harsh

and shrill. I looked up toward the east. There in the middle of that vast ridge were the dark figures of the two murderers, still far away but coming fast. They must have seen the ice axe when I dropped it. The chrome.

Now I didn't even stop to think. Pushing off from the cliff face, I swung back out into space and let go. The snow was soft and wet, but I landed hard enough in a shower of snow crystals and light. I struggled to my feet, gasping for breath as more yells from above echoed faintly across the mountain-side. Looking up I saw the two men through the tangle of hair and bandanna and snow that covered my eyes. They were still little more than dots against the snow, but already it seemed that I could hear their panting as I had heard it only hours before. One of the men seemed bigger than the other, and was in the lead. I looked quickly around me and found the ice axe buried up to the pick in snow. I pulled it up, grabbed it around the shaft, and started down the steep slope as fast as I could go.

The snow was very soft, reaching above my ankles when I stepped in it. I tried to hurry, but it seemed impossible to do without slipping. I kept on, dropping heel first into the steeply banked snow, letting gravity do as much of the work as possible. It was agonizingly slow, and my only consolation was that the two men behind were having the same problem.

Another long, wailing cry broke forth from above and lingered in the rocks with a dozen chilling echoes. I glanced back. The two men had come down past the lower east end of the summit rampart, on approximately the same path I wanted to take to avoid going down the cliff. As I watched, one of the men fell on the snow, and what appeared to be a rifle slipped from his grasp and went sliding down the slope. In its futile way the sight made me feel better.

The man above shouted again, long and insistently.

"Aliiii! Aliiii!" Perhaps the name of one of the men on the west side. They were out of earshot for the moment, but they wouldn't be for long.

I hurried on, holding the ice axe to the side, not even attempting to use it in the soft snow. Below me, the cloud bank held the mountain in its embrace, offering shelter and a gray, shadowy anonymity, if only I could reach it. Down in those rocks, in the midst of that shifting fog, my chances could only get better.

"Aliiii!" Again the man above shouted. "Aliiii!" And with every echo I came closer to the clouds.

But suddenly there was another echo, another *voice*, longer, lower, more distant than that from above, coming from far below and to the left. I went even faster, descending in one continuous motion, relying upon the depth of the snow and my boots to hold me.

"Aliii!"

And an almost inaudible answer came from below, from the men who would try to close the net. The voice above went on, calling out in distant, guttural phrases fraught with unreality and menace.

I reached out with my right heel and went sprawling in the snow. I had slipped on a shallow spot where rock and melted ice had undermined my footing. I started to slide, and caught myself with the pick of the ice axe. I began to curse myself, for I realized that all along I could have been glissading down this torturous slope as we had done the previous afternoon. Instead I had been punishing my knees for nothing.

I shoved off down the slope, using the ice axe as an emergency brake, sliding wildly toward the cloud bank and its beckoning gray mist. Big, bigger, impossibly huge, the clouds loomed above me: nebulous giants guarding the portals of hell. But now ironically they were my only hope of escape as I slid toward the rockfall on the seat of my pants. I was almost there. The slope leveled off slightly, and I coasted to a halt. All the crevices in my clothing and boots were crammed with snow and ice. I got to my feet and marched on toward the gray.

There were rocks now, random, jagged boulders that had partly emerged from the snow cover. They hinted at the pile of rubble beneath: a massive graveyard of all the rock that had fallen from the summit over the centuries. High above me, the leading edge of the cloud bank had begun to close in over my view of the summit. As I passed the jagged tip of a rock and walked into the shadow, I looked back for a final time at the summit of Hasan Gazi. In that unearthly scene of beauty and violence the loudest sound was still the rush of breath in my throat. In the distance the two killers continued their headlong dash down the snowfield, but they were still far out of range as I took ten seconds to gaze at the mountain that had drawn me for so long. It stood there as massive, white, and magnificent as ever. An involuntary spasm of pain gripped the hollow of my throat as I turned downhill and pressed on into the mist.

From what I had seen, the men were no more than five minutes behind me, if that. Soon I heard them yelling again, now out of sight in the sunlight I had left behind. And below on the left, but slightly closer now, a two-syllable cry I could not comprehend.

Before long I had penetrated the heart of the cloud and headed slightly east to avoid the men coming from the west ridge. Visibility was down to perhaps twenty or thirty yards, as in a heavy fog. I had seen from above, however, that the cloud mass was anything but even, and from time to time I entered areas of clearing, where the clouds parted in an aura of blinding, unearthly white haze. Without the sun and with the fog around me, I shivered beneath my down jacket, my breathing becoming increasingly labored as I searched agonizingly for a way to make my feet move faster over the rocks. But my attempts proved more and more futile as I descended from the broad expanse of the snowfield into the lower regions with their heaps of boulders fallen from the summit over the centuries. Lost in the fog, with men coming at me from two directions, I could only pick my way over the boulders with a slowness that made me want to cry out in frustration. The boulders were huge, covered with pockmarks the size of half dollars, and splintered jaggedly along the edges. Deep in the crevices between them I could see patches of dark, melting snow, and occasionally I heard the soft gurgle of water.

More shouts from behind were answered from the left. The men on the snowfield sounded closer, but those coming from the west seemed to be about the same distance away. They were having the same problem I had had on the rocks, and with their leather boots maybe worse.

And the game went on, quietly and relentlessly. Occasionally the pursuers would cry out to each other, but to anyone watching, the race would have seemed to pass by in a vacuum. Low, impassioned breathing, the scuffle of Vibram against rock, a weak mutter of frustration as the ice axe tip slipped again with a tinny scrape, but other than that, silence.

I scrambled over a rock the size of an auto and leaped to the next one, three feet away across a shallow gap. It rocked precariously, and I had to shift violently to avoid a fall. The cloud cover opened up again and suffused the scene with a white glare, as in an unfocused and overexposed film. But my vision was temporarily extended, and straight ahead I could see the dim outline of a massive rock, black and looming in the mist. To the right of it and beyond, as I moved toward the east, the terrain seemed to level out a little with smaller rocks, perhaps a third the size of those I had just traversed. I moved on, faster now, determined to stay ahead.

From the sound of the cries I knew I had kept the same distance from my pursuers. Judging from their shouts, however, the left-hand pair were no longer below me; we seemed to be just about parallel with each other. If true, this meant that I was on the verge of escaping from the net. The west group could no longer cut me off, and if the clouds held, I might get ahead and stay there. But if we came out of the clouds, I felt sure they would start shooting, and shooting to kill this time. Still, I was fairly certain that the cloud cover would hold. Surely I hadn't come down to the level of the tomb yet, and I knew there would be clouds almost to that level, if not beyond. So there was a chance, a good chance, and as I ran on down the mountain hope rushed through me like a surge of adrenalin. I pushed myself even harder, leaping from rock to rock, frantic with the thought that I might actually make it.

Soon I came upon another awesome boulder, this one as big as a truck, looming black above me in the mist. It must have fallen almost three thousand feet down the mountainside before coming to rest at that place. I skirted it, angling down and toward the east.

Coming round the boulder, I picked up the pace again, leaping across a five-foot gap between one rock and the next. It was a long jump on such a precariously piled heap of rocks, and five seconds later I had cause to regret it. As my left boot landed on the rock, it rolled crazily with my weight. I tried to compensate, but it was too late. With a bruising, flesh-scraping thump I fell onto the rock, my foot thrusting deep into the crevices beneath.

I cursed bitterly under my breath and managed to sit upright, noting with disgust the red and torn patches where skin had been flayed from my hands. My left foot remained stuck, jammed into a crevice between the rocks, and as the initial shock of the fall passed I could feel pain shoot up my leg when I moved it slightly. Gasping for breath, I cursed again. The ankle seemed to be twisted.

In the mist the man called again. Closer this time. Using the ice axe, still looped to my right wrist, I pulled myself out of the sitting position. I tugged slightly on the imprisoned foot, and the pain took my breath away. I saw a tiny feather float off in the breeze and realized that the right sleeve of my precious down jacket had been torn open by the rock.

There were more cries from behind. With a violent wrench I pulled my foot loose. This time the pain was too much, and I cried out. Immediately I regretted my cry, for the killers had heard, and they started conversing again in shouts.

Again I started to move, but I could only limp along now, favoring my right foot. It was very painful, for every time I moved the rocks seemed to shift beneath me, and the necessity of keeping my balance nearly drove me mad with pain. By this time the men were shouting back and forth in virtually continuous conversation, and their high-pitched, excited voices seemed closer than they had been. I veered off even more sharply toward the east, thinking they would probably expect me to head more or less straight down. I had to try anything at this point, since I could no longer match their speed. I limped on through the wilderness of rock moving almost parallel with the contours of the north face. The clouds hung thicker than ever, and I was grateful for that much luck at least.

Soon a loud, angry cry of pain erupted from very close behind me, at almost the same place where I had fallen only minutes before. I wondered which of them had fallen and why. How they must have cursed themselves for letting me get away earlier in the morning. But they were closing the distance between us, and if they were clever and decided to spread out across the mountain instead of moving in twos, I knew it would all be over.

I hobbled along, making my way over a low heap of rock, and suddenly was confronted with another snow-filled couloir, a massive river of white flowing out of and disappearing into the vapor along the mountainside. I couldn't see the other side in the heavy mist.

Gingerly, tentatively, I climbed down off the rock and out onto the snow. I advanced slowly toward the middle of the trough and then stopped. There, beneath me in the haze, faint yet unmistakable, I could see the furrows carved by Sinan and me as we slid down the mountain less than twenty-four hours before. Quickly I looked downhill to the left, and there they were: the blurred but lasting footprints left behind as we scrambled happily into the warmth and sunlight. I could barely contain the sob that rose like acid in my throat. Over there in the rocks I knew the water was gushing. *To the Tigris. To Baghdad.* I limped across the couloir and over the rubble heaped along the east edge.

At last I had come full circle, and as I staggered, exhausted, across the north face where yesterday's fantasies had been born and consumed, I knew that at least one of the players was with me again, his face blank, stalking through the fluid, anonymous mist. Since the killers had spied me at the bottom of the rappel, events had accelerated like those of an old movie cranked up beyond the limits of comprehension. The slide down the snowfield, the escape into the clouds, the painstaking descent through the rockfall, the twisted ankle, all had become a headlong blur of action punctuated by hoarse panting and the chink of my ice axe against the rock. And now I knew that the nightmare was flickering madly toward the end as the twenty-one frames per second became twenty-five and the twenty-five twenty-eight, and with every frame the movement of a muscle, the meeting of boot with soil, the shock of another spasm from my left ankle. Far ahead in the grayness the cloud began to transform itself slowly and in a ghostlike way before my eyes. Out of the fluid mass something white and unearthly had been born, a sauntering, malignant phantasm spawned in a crevice of mountain rock and come forth to smear my flesh forever into the soil. I limped toward it transfixed, hoping that all would end, that my life would vaporize, as in a dream, but the wraith was only sunlight and fantasy, and I passed through it untouched.

But back in the shifting vapor a voice cried out in excited, commanding words, lower, more guttural than any I had heard up to then. A strange voice, seemingly alone, coming from what sounded like the other side of the couloir. Surely the four had at last spread out across the mountain, and this one, covering the east, had discovered my tracks in the snow.

I tried to go faster, but the ankle wouldn't let me. I came to the long snowdrift I remembered from the day before and crossed it in despair, knowing that my footprints would soon be discovered. I pressed on, minutes away from the beginnings of the rock maze. The low voice shouted again, even closer behind me, and the answers came back in successively diminishing volume from across the mountain. A boulder loomed in the mist. I hurried by, noticing the blotches indicating where moss had once grown and died. Another boulder . . . and another. And minutes later I was in the phantasmagoria of black rocks and pillars, long ago vomited from the earth and left to blacken and erode on the mountainside. I cut down and over, down and over the same path as yesterday. And on through the narrow defiles between the rocks toward the tomb, that heap of rubble whose core had been beyond my touch, beyond my least comprehension.

I limped from behind the last boulder and saw the ruin below me in the secondary crater, almost invisible behind the curtain of mist. I stared for a second then flinched at the shock of my lead pursuer's brutal voice shouting behind me.

I looked back and almost choked with despair. Enlightened at last, I now saw the marks that would lead him to me: the neat, distinctive punctures made in the soil by the tip of my ice axe. I was horrified at the realization of my own carelessness.

In the rocks I could hear the faint sound of clumsy, uneven steps and the sliding rattle of dislodged scree. I retraced my steps and flattened myself against one of the monoliths along the trail, exactly the place where the monster had waited the previous afternoon. I brought my ice axe to eye level and looked at it: chrome moly steel, a reasonable point, with medium serrations along the pick. It certainly could penetrate ice, but flesh? . . . I would have one chance, right after he passed me, in his back, between the left shoulder blade and the spine. The passage at that point was only six feet wide. I raised the ice axe above me and held it there, all the while trembling like the bearer of a ritual offering.

The steps grew louder and more distinct behind me. They slowed, then stopped. I was frozen against the rock, the axe upraised. *What is he doing? Why can't he follow a simple trail? Maybe he's looking in the rocks. For what? The fool!* The footsteps came on again slowly, and then faster: one . . . two . . . three, four, five . . . six. They stopped once more, and now I could hear him breathing in the grayness behind me.

"Hasa-a-an!" The low roar of his voice shook my body and squeezed the fear from inside. It oozed wet and sticky down the inside of my thighs.

The man behind me was answered from far away in the middle of the mountain, and he called back in a loud, commanding voice. I waited. There was one beat of silence, then a step, another, and a boot scuffing on stone, then another, and my arms wanted to melt as the steps became louder and then became a living thing with black boots. . . .

"Aaaa!"

With a cry I propelled the pick into the upper left quadrant of the dark-jacketed back. The man, somewhat shorter than I, stiffened as if shot through with electricity, his head and arms wrenching back as the massive bolt-action rifle he carried dropped to the ground with a clatter. But as soon as the gun dropped, he tried to bend over with the ice axe lodged in his back. Standing behind him, my hands still on the shaft, I didn't know what to do. He was supposed to die, but he hadn't. Keeping my left hand on the shaft and putting my right against the adze, I dug the pick into him, trying to wrench him up and away from the gun. The steel made a disgusting sound as it twisted inside him, but still no blood came. The man became upright with his arms held out and his mouth opened in soundless, uncomprehending horror. I still could not fully see his face, but he was caught, hooked, held by the serrations and his own muscular spasms.

Once more he tried to reach down, and this time I pushed him toward the edge of the crater, trying to get him past his own gun. He stumbled forward a few steps and then stopped as he attempted to resist my pushing. This only forced the pick in deeper. I was up against him, clinging desperately to the metal protruding from his back. He wouldn't die. I pushed him again. The serrations on the adze had made bloody punctures in the heel of my right hand.

He stumbled several steps toward the edge of the crater, then seemed to gather himself together, refusing to budge against all my efforts. With a low cry, he whirled and with one incredibly violent movement wrenched himself free of my grasp. We stood face to face for the first time, and almost with relief I saw that he was not the faceless monster I had met the day before. His face was that of a peasant: unshaven, brown, with a long, black moustache and eyes that glared at me in suffering and rage. The axe still hung from his back, though it had been wrenched askew by the sudden movement. He swayed there before me, close to the edge of the crater, his features paralyzed by the magnitude of his effort. I took a step back from him, but before I could react he had produced a knife and slashed me violently on the left arm. A sudden spurt of blood ran down the back of my hand, and I could see that the down jacket had been sliced open. I sprang back out of range, but he started again for me, holding the knife out with its blade upturned.

But two steps were all that he took. He faltered, then stopped and gazed upward as if his head were being pulled back by an invisible wire. At last I saw what was the matter. Out of his back, down the shaft of the ice axe, and thence to the ground, there gushed what seemed to be a river of blood. The twisting and wrenching had done their job: the pick had worked its way through to his heart.

The man died slowly. He sank to his knees as if in prayer. Then, still clutching the knife, his eyes staring blankly into the mist, he tottered and finally fell face down onto the rocky ground. The ice axe still clung to his back, and from the puncture it had made there poured a ghastly spring of dark, glistening blood.

I limped over to the body and stood looking at it for a long, unfeeling minute. Untying the bandanna from my forehead I reached down and used it to swab the blood from the shaft of my ice axe. I dropped the red cloth on the ground and noticed the smears it had left on my hands. In the middle of my slashed left arm the down had become matted with blood as hundreds of tiny white feathers streamed into the gray mist. I grasped the ice axe and felt the stickiness along the varnished shaft. Then slowly, inch by inch, I pulled the pick up and out of his body. It was a sound like the soft ending of love. I held the axe before me and watched the dark liquid flow along the metal and drip slowly from the end. I remembered a TV film of *Macbeth* seen long ago as a child, especially the image of a hairy, barbaric Macduff standing in a room at the end of a dark castle hall hacking and hacking at the head of his enemy, consuming his hatred in destruction. I stood there hypnotized by the memory, numbed by the catharsis, fascinated by a globule of blood that was poised coagulating at the point of the ice axe. I turned the pick toward me as a strange, forgotten longing stirred at the tip of my tongue. My mouth opened slightly, and the globule moved to within an inch of my lips. I felt the crust along them, dry and cracked. The tongue moved forward in my mouth, a thing apart, reaching, reaching . . . with a cry I spat into the ground.

But now there were footsteps, loud scuffs of leather, and I looked up to see the giant who had pursued me that morning running at me from out of the rocks. I brought up the ice axe to strike, but the man parried the blow with his left arm, tore the ice axe from me, and sent it clattering against a rock. He grabbed me by my jacket and threw me over against the rounded surface of a nearby rock. There was a holstered revolver on his right hip. I kicked at him, but the high black boots he wore made my efforts futile. He had a cloth wrapped around his right hand, and on his face were the four dark punctures left by my crampons. He pinioned my arms and body then began hitting me hard with the flat of his hand. My head snapped back and forth and bounced hard against the rock. Pinioning my torso with his left arm he pushed my legs up and tried to wrench my jeans off using his right hand. I twisted and struggled and kicked out against him. He hit me, again and again, and I blacked out momentarily.

When I came to seconds later he was on me, reaching for me, his grimacing face inches away. His grip on my right arm had relaxed. It was practically free. My fingers touched the points of the instep crampons, still dangling from the belt loop. I relaxed slightly, and he slid in. I cried out from the pain, but I knew he was mine. He was on top of me, trapped. The crampon strap came free, and one set of the points fell into my right hand. His grip relaxed further as he stared into the mist. He raised his head slightly to look at me, and with a sudden wrench of my body I raked the crampons hard and deep across his face and into his left eye.

Crying out in pain, he reached for the eye. I lunged at him again, but he parried the blow and began pummeling me even harder than before. Again and again he hit me, and I felt my mouth filling with warm blood. I started to black out.

There was a scurrying sound and a low gasp, and suddenly he withdrew. I looked up through my daze and saw that there were now two faces directly in front of me. My attacker stood grimacing in surprise, his left eye streaming blood, and his hands clutching desperately at a red bandanna that was now wrapped tightly around his throat. At his left shoulder, straining hard at the garrote, was the man whom yesterday I had called a monster.

I got down off the rock as the scarred man pulled his captive slowly backward toward the edge of the crater. He had him around the neck, but the contest was by no means over. The larger man was very strong, and the tendons of his neck were holding well against the arms of his attacker. He gagged desperately, searching for breath. Scarface tightened the noose even further, but still the big man would not go down.

I limped toward them. The big man was a horrifying, sickening sight as he stood there with his legs apart straining against death. I hated him with a purity I had never known before. Weighted by the revolver the man's trousers had fallen to his knees, and as he fought against the ever-tightening bandanna his genitals hung impotent and useless beneath him. I took three more limping steps forward and delivered my right boot hard into the middle of his crotch. He went down, and minutes later he was dead.

Scarface got to his feet and for a moment we looked at each other. I'm sure there was as little expression on my face as there was on his. Facing that man in those clouds, I felt as if I were in another world. He still held my bandanna, and I put out my hand, asking to have it back. He hesitated, then looked down and placed it in my palm. I took it and tied it loosely around my neck.

"Hasa-a-an!" A cry from back in the rocks.

The man and I looked at each other, and he motioned toward the crater: *away, away.* I shook my head, no. I wasn't going to run anywhere.

"Hasa-a-an!" Closer now, the voice came from near the beginning of the maze.

The man looked back into the rocks, then at me. I didn't move. Finally he called out in a hoarse voice:

"Gel! Gel!"

He pointed excitedly to the big man's revolver, and I bent to pull it from its holster. Scarface picked up the first man's rifle, then rummaged in the dead owner's jacket pocket for some more ammunition. I heard the sounds of running feet behind us in the fog. My head throbbed, and my throat was parched. But it was coming to an end. For better or for worse, it would all end soon.

We took positions in the rocks, I in the same place as before and Scarface on the other side of the path. He made low noises at me, and I saw him gesture in the direction from which the men were coming. From my crevice in the rock I nodded yes, we would try to shoot them there.

I could hear them now, two men running close together through the rocks. They were laughing.

"Hasan!" the yell came, and I heard a low acknowledgment from the boulders above.

As I crouched there holding the cocked revolver with both hands, I realized what a poor position I was in. I could see virtually nothing of the trail. Every time my heart beat, the gun barrel seemed to move. I couldn't see how I would ever hit anything with it. I tried to steady it against the rock, but that helped only a little.

The men were nearly upon us. Their footsteps and voices grew louder and louder. The black rock wavered before me at the end of the gun barrel.

No one appeared for a long, silent second. Then a rifle shot exploded from the rocks above me, followed by a shout of agony off to the right. Scarface had started firing before I could see anything. There was another deafening report close on the first, and then another ringing harshly off the rocks. There was noise everywhere, and I could see nothing.

I got to my feet and crept forward, peeking around the edge of the rock. There was another explosion from the rocks where Scarface was hiding. I saw the bullet ricochet off a large rock only twenty yards away. Crouched at its base and protected from the shots coming from above was a dark, bearded peasant wearing a dirty white turban and a bandolier of ammunition. He was looking up into the rocks with his rifle at the ready. Beside him, his partner was sprawled full-length on the ground.

I heard shouts and looked up to see Scarface motioning me to move back. He raised himself slightly from his hiding place, and there was another rifle shot that caught him in the face, spinning him out of sight between the rocks.

The man with the turban was very quick and efficient. He had already pulled back the rifle bolt as I turned toward him. Raising my pistol, I heard him ram the bolt home on another cartridge. And as I pulled the trigger, with the sight wavering crazily before me, the barrel of his rifle was rising swiftly to confront me.

The two weapons went off simultaneously. I fell backward from the kick and felt something like a hot iron scorch my left cheek. When the smoke cleared I was still holding the revolver, and the man was slumped against his rock ten yards away.

I got up slowly and moved toward the rock, holding the gun before me fully cocked. The bearded man was still alive, but wouldn't be for long. Just above his heart was a hole the size of an apple, and out of it his life's blood now flowed, spreading its stain across his dirty blue shirt. I walked up to him and gazed down numbly. While I watched him the man opened his eyes and seemed to come alive again. His dark eyes saw me, lighting up in recognition. His right hand rose in greeting and a smile of real affection spread its shining arc across a mouthful of gold teeth. He held the smile for some seconds, then closed his eyes and moved no more.

I turned away and discovered that my own jacket was wet with blood. Feeling my left cheek, I discovered the deep gouge left by the bullet. I could almost stick my tongue through it.

I went to look for Scarface and found him, as I had feared, facedown at the base of a boulder. I didn't turn him over, but from the condition of the back of his head it was obvious that the shot had been one more insult to the face Allah had given him. I wanted to cry, but somehow I couldn't.

I limped out of the rocks and shuffled slowly toward the edge of the secondary crater, past the two bodies already there. The bleeding from my cheek had slowed. The gash on my arm had been stanched with goose down, and the delicate plumes continued to float off across the mountain. I came to the edge of the crater and saw the tomb below me, silent and welcoming at last. I knelt there on the ground and wept. Far down the mountain I could hear the voices of men, distant and questioning.

MICHAEL CROSSMAN

Saturday morning, July 28, I was awakened around 7:30 by my doorbell. When I opened the door I found a man waiting with an express telegram. I gave him a tip, thanked him, and closed the door.

The telegram was from Tatvan, and it was in Turkish. It said that Julia was badly hurt and asked if I could come to help. No details, just that. The name at the end was Kemal Altay. I read it again: "Julia badly hurt. Please come Tatvan." It looked ominous, I must say. From what I knew of Julia, she had to be pretty badly hurt to require any help from me. Then I thought of the mountain and of that region and its reputation. Suddenly I was very frightened.

I went to the phone and called up a travel agency I often use in Bebek. There was no answer, of course, at that time of the morning. Going into my office I started rummaging through the drawers: I had a Turkish Airlines schedule somewhere.

After several minutes of clumsy and frantic searching I

finally came up with a two-year-old schedule. Well, I could only hope it hadn't been revised. I looked toward the back and—yes, they did have a flight to Van on Saturday. Two years ago they did anyway. Leaving from Ankara at eleven o'clock. If I moved fast I could get a shuttle from Yeşilköy that would get me there on time. Ten minutes later I was down on the street looking for a taxi.

I won't bother giving the details of the rest of that day—the traffic jams, the endless hassles at the ticket counter, and the rest of it. Suffice it to say that around four o'clock in the afternoon, due to modern technology and a lot of old-fashioned luck, I was on the THY F–27 as it touched down at the Van airstrip.

There was no bus to Tatvan, so I had to hire a taxi. We were in the car, riding along, when the driver asked me if I had heard about the murders in Tanyeri.

"Murders? What murders?!"

"Seven people killed," he said. "The police have an American woman. They say she did it."

"What!" *Holy Jesus.*

"Yes, a woman. Isn't that funny?"

"What happened?"

He shrugged. "I don't know. Seven people killed. An American woman."

"Impossible!"

"Well, it happened."

"That's impossible, man. How could an American woman kill seven Turks?"

He hesitated, as if to say that he hadn't considered that part of it.

"You're right," he said. "I don't know. Maybe they were Kurds!" He laughed a lot at this witticism.

I knew right away that he had to be talking about Julia. How many American women could there be in Tanyeri? His

164

story was untrue, of course. It had to be. But true or not, I've never heard of *anybody* having a sweet time with the Turkish authorities. If Julia was suspected of *anything* she was in trouble. Oh Jesus. I looked off at the lake as we wound along the shoreline. The big white ship was just completing its late afternoon run into Van from the other end. Süphan Dagh rose in glory above it all. I was scared shitless.

We got into Tatvan a little after six. I found a hotel and then had dinner at a restaurant on the main square. After that I went looking for the local police station.

I found it up a side street, a plain two-story building looking dumpy and bureaucratic in the gathering twilight. I walked in and talked to a man in a police uniform sitting behind a desk. He looked somewhat surprised when I started speaking Turkish but soon brightened up and became quite helpful. I asked him if he knew about the deaths at Tanyeri, and he said yes of course. I told him I was here to find a friend that was involved and gave him the name of Kemal Altay.

"Ah yes, Kemal Bey," he said, "the professor!"

"Yes, that's right. Where can I find him?"

He gave me the name of a hotel that was very close to my own.

"Do they have the American woman there?" I asked.

"Yes, she is there. Very badly injured."

"What happened? Is there going to be trouble?" I asked somewhat diffidently. I definitely did not want to ask any more questions than I had to.

"There will be an official inquiry tomorrow," the policeman said, somewhat more soberly. "Nobody knows anything now." I thanked him for the help and left.

The hotel he had mentioned was right on the city square. There was a policeman sitting outside the entrance, and he looked up suspiciously as I walked in. At the desk I inquired for Professor Kemal Altay, and the clerk pointed over my right shoulder. I turned and saw a lounge area where a man and woman were sitting. The man was small and rather handsome, with dark, curly hair. The woman, obviously foreign, wore glasses and had straight, dark hair that fell over her shoulders. They seemed rather lost as I walked up.

"Excuse me," I asked the man in Turkish, "are you Professor Altay?"

"Yes!" he answered in English, rising from his chair, "are you Julia's friend from Istanbul?"

"Yes, I'm Mike Crossman."

"Good, good! I'm very happy you could come. This is Mary." He indicated the girl, who smiled in greeting.

"Glad to meet you," I said.

"I was afraid you wouldn't get the telegram in time to take the plane," Kemal said. "I sent it as soon as we arrived here last night."

"Yes, I had quite a time, but I made it."

We sat down. They were drinking tea, and I ordered some as well. There was a pause before I asked the inevitable question.

"Kemal Bey, can you please tell me what happened? I don't know anything. How is Julia?"

They exchanged a where-on-earth-do-we-begin look, and then Mary answered, "Julia is upstairs in her room now sleeping. She's been there most of the day. I have to tell you she is in pretty bad shape. She has a gash on her cheek, bruises on her hands and face, another cut on her arm, and a sprained ankle."

"But how? How did all this happen?"

They proceeded to tell me the whole grisly story from Julia's departure on Wednesday to her discovery by two peasants early Friday afternoon. It was simply incredible to me.

"But who were these men?" I asked at the end. "Why did they do it? For money?"

"Partly for that," Mary replied, "but also we think for revenge."

"Revenge?"

"To repay an insult. One of the attackers—the leader, we think—used to work for us. He was from Gaziova, the Kurdish village near Tanyeri. He had a grudge against Sinan, who was the young man with Julia. They had a fight about three weeks ago, the day Julia arrived in Tanyeri, actually."

"It was a stupid fight," Kemal said in a low and bitter voice. "It blew up over nothing, and now Sinan is dead." He was near tears. The two of them were obviously devastated, and I could hardly blame them. Still it seemed totally incomprehensible: two men murdered and a woman slashed and beaten all because of one peasant's petty vendetta.

"What happened to the two men Julia went with? Will you try and send the American's body home?"

"No, we buried both Sinan and Frank at the castle," Mary said. "We discussed it and decided that it's probably what they would have wanted. The other men were all buried in Gaziova. All but one."

"Which?"

"The man that Julia said saved her life. They buried him on the mountain."

"Who was he?"

"A freak," Mary said. "No face. Destroyed by something."

"I inquired about him in the village," Kemal said. "He lived up on the mountain, tending sheep sometimes and begging. They wouldn't let him stay in the village."

"What happened to his face?"

"Nobody seemed to know for sure. Some said an accident when he was in the army. But it could have been a lot of things. He was crazy, they say."

"Of course." A pause. I sipped the last of my tea.

"Well, what happens now?" I asked.

"Well, tomorrow we have the official inquiry at ten," Kemal replied. "The *kaymakam* will be there and other people too." (The *kaymakam* is like a county governor, a big man in town.)

"Do you think there will be trouble?"

"There is always trouble with the officials. But they say the *kaymakam* is a good man."

"Will Julia be formally accused?"

"I don't think so, why?" I told him what the taxi driver had said. "I'm sure you know, Mike," Kemal said, verbalizing my misgivings, "there is no telling what these petty bureaucrats will do."

"I know."

"I have a certain amount of influence," he continued, "and in the end I'm sure everything will turn out all right. But they could make it difficult if they want to."

"Of course. Is Julia under arrest now? I saw a policeman outside."

"No, not formally under arrest. But they have confiscated her passport and stationed the policeman there."

"Oh."

"So what's the difference, right?"

"Right."

Kemal brought out his hands palms up in the traditional gesture of resignation and despair. And he was right; we could do nothing but wait and hope. I knew I had a sleepless night ahead of me.

The next morning I walked into the hotel and found Kemal, Mary, and Julia in the lounge. Julia was sitting with her back toward me as I walked over, and when I saw her face I almost fell apart.

"Hello, Mike," she said, her low voice sunk almost to a whisper.

"Hello."

We kissed, and I gripped her shoulders to steady myself as I stood there surveying the damage. Her face was wrapped in bandages, and the parts that were not covered had swollen to the point where she could barely see. Her left arm was bandaged, and her left ankle had been set in a cast. Only her blond hair and red bandanna remained unchanged. I must have looked as horrified as I felt because she looked at me and said quietly, "Don't worry, Mike, I'm all right."

"Well, I am worried," I managed to say weakly, "we're all worried."

"Come on, sit down. I'm sorry you had to come out here. But I'm glad to see you."

"I think you'll want someone to help with that pack now."

"I suppose so. If everything gets finished this morning, I can leave tomorrow. I think I'm ready to leave," she said softly, ending with an ironic smile.

"I'm sure everything will go smoothly," Kemal said. "I talked to the police again late last night, and they seemed to think there would be no trouble."

"Where will the inquest be held?" I asked.

"At the police station."

"You said the *kaymakam* will be there?"

"Yes, that is what they said."

"Will he conduct it?"

"No, the public prosecutor will do that. He speaks English, I understand, that's why he is doing it. The *kaymakam* understands a little bit also."

After a few more minutes the guard came in with instructions that we were to proceed to the police station. We got up and left, with Julia holding my arm and the other two in front. The people on the street stopped and stared at us as we walked along, especially at Julia with her bandages. We were, to be sure, a dismal little caravan.

We entered the police building and were taken into a room with chairs lined up in rows facing the back wall. There was a small table, obviously set up for the magistrate, and to the right of it a chair for the witnesses. Above the magistrate's table hung my favorite Atatürk picture: the one where he has a moustache and looks sensitive and concerned. The room had been painted so long before as to make its color irrelevant. It was all very grim. We sat down on the right side and waited. Of the four of us, Julia was the only one who didn't look nervous. I guess after all she had been through she figured nothing could hurt her now.

There was no one else in the room when we entered, but soon they started drifting in: a few policemen, peasants, and others in city clothes. They sat down and mumbled to each other as they stared at us. At last some rather official-looking types entered the room, and Kemal, sitting in the aisle seat, got up to greet them. It was very cordial for a few minutes as they all bowed and shook hands. One of the men especially, a fortyish, short, clean-shaven man, seemed quite friendly. The dark-suited man with him, however, was appreciably more reserved. He had a moustache and was carrying a very proper-looking briefcase. In addition to these two there were other hangers-on, a mixed group in uniforms and civilian clothes. They passed on to the front of the room and sat down. The short, clean-shaven man sat at the table under the Atatürk picture, while his colleague laid his briefcase down on the table and proceeded to take out some papers.

Kemal leaned over and informed us that the man behind the table was the *kaymakam*. Because of his interest in the incident, and because it was merely a police inquest, he had decided to preside. The man with the moustache was the prosecutor who would be asking the questions. Both he and the *kaymakam* spoke a little English.

After a few minutes the prosecutor cleared his throat and barked out the name of the first witness, a forlorn little peasant who was evidently one of the two men who had found Julia early Friday afternoon. I didn't understand all of the questions and answers during the ensuing interrogation, but it was obvious that the prosecutor was really running him through the wringer. The poor peasant sat there and cowered in his rags as the official hurled question after question at him in a loud accusatory tone. He seemed to be trying his best to implicate this man and his friend as accessories, but the peasant stuck to his story: he had only been up there to look after his fields when he heard shooting and went to look. At last, after a brief consultation with the *kaymakam*, the prosecutor dismissed him, and he went back to his seat amid mutters from the spectators.

The next witness was Kemal himself. As soon as he took his seat in the witness chair, we could see an immediate change in the demeanor of the prosecutor, who no longer played the lofty government official browbeating some swine of a peasant. His questions now came forth mellifluously and with the highest respect. Mary and I exchanged a mildly nauseated look. When did you hear about the trouble? he asked. What did you do? Do you know this American woman who was found? Why do you think the murders happened? Kemal answered smoothly and deferentially to all the questions: he had received word Friday afternoon; he had met Julia coming down and heard her story; they had brought the bodies down Friday night and left for Tatvan as soon as possible. He repeated Mary's reasons for the murders: revenge and money. Both the prosecutor and the *kaymakam* thanked Kemal profusely, and he came back to his seat.

"Miss Julia Warren!" the prosecutor barked in a heavy accent. She stood up and made her way slowly to the witness chair. The room suddenly became very quiet. I think everyone there was holding his breath. In spite of her bruised face Julia was easily the most dignified, self-possessed person there. She didn't look nearly as apprehensive as I felt. By that time I had decided that the prosecutor was unpredictable at best and probably a real son of a bitch. The examination began, and I soon found out how right I was.

"You are Miss Julia Warren?" The man spoke commandingly, with a great sense of self-importance.

"Yes."

"For how long have you been in Turkey, Miss Julia?"

"Exactly four weeks."

"For what reason did you come here?"

"To work at Tanyeri."

"With Kemal Bey?"

"Yes."

"You are a student?"

"No."

"But you came to work? Why?"

"For a vacation. For fun."

"For fun?" He made it sound like an accusation.

"Yes," she answered quietly. I could see her bridle.

"When did you begin to climb the Hasan Gazi mountain?"

"Wednesday afternoon."

"And when was your plan to come back?"

"Friday afternoon."

"When did your friends die?"

"I think Thursday night."

"You think? You do not know?"

"It was Thursday night. I found them dead when I woke up Friday morning."

"But you were alive. Why?"

"I don't know."

"How did you not hear anything?"

"I was asleep."

"You were asleep. You did not wake up? This is incredible."

"We'd been climbing for two days."

"Why did you kill your friends?"

I could see Julia trying to control her anger as she stared at him and withheld any answer. Kemal and I glanced at each other. We were getting a real lesson in applied xenophobia.

"Why did you kill your friends?!" he repeated, louder.

"I did not."

"I think you did it."

"I did not." It was a simple, quiet statement.

"Who killed them?"

"The four men who came after me, I presume."

"What four men?"

"I saw them when I got up. I saw them running up the mountain. I went to tell Sinan and Frank and found them dead."

"Then you did what?"

"I ran."

"Up the mountain?"

"Yes."

"These men followed you?"

"Yes."

"How have you escaped?"

"From the summit I went down the middle, and they came after me."

"But they caught you?"

"Yes, they caught me in the rocks by the tomb."

"How did you get away?"

"I killed the first one with my ice axe."

"How?"

"With my ice axe."

"What? What is this thing?"

Kemal broke in at this point and supplied a brief account in Turkish of the appearance and function of a mountaineer's ice axe. The prosecutor responded with much thanks and an unctuous smile. Then he went back to the questions.

"How did you kill the first man with this thing?"

"I got him in the back."

"What? You killed him before he had seen you?"

"Yes."

"So you have murdered this man."

"No."

"But you hit him in the back."

"Yes, but he was after me."

"How do you know this?"

"Are you serious? They had killed my friends and chased me all over the mountain."

"Yes, yes, of course." He was very skeptical. "What about the three other men?"

"A second man came after I had killed the first, but he was killed by another man, a man who came along and helped me."

"Who is this other man?"

"He was a man who evidently lived up there."

"On the mountain?"

"Yes. He was scarred. An outcast from the village."

"Yes, of course. Why did the second man attack you?"

"To rape me."

"Did you have congress with this man?"

"Conegrates? I don't—"

"Congress, congress."

"Oh you mean—what?"

"Congress, sexual congress."

"Why?"

"I ask the questions please."

She didn't answer.

"Did you have congress?"

"Yes!" She spat it at him low and hard.

"You have allowed him?"

"No."

"Yes, of course. Did you give him reason to do this thing?"

"Of course not."

"You have killed his friend, yes?"

"Yes."

"Is that not good reason to attack someone?" He looked as if he had just proved the existence of God.

"How did your friend kill the second man?"

"With this." She pointed to the bandanna in her hair.

"This red cloth? How?"

"By strangling. I left it on the ground and the man picked it up and attacked the other as he was attacking me."

"And you are wearing it? You are wearing this thing?! Why?!"

"I'm wearing it because it's mine."

"Yes, of course." He turned away and walked to the left side of the room. The *kaymakam* looked a bit worried at this point. I don't think he really understood what the prosecutor was doing. The questioning continued.

"You say four men have followed you, Miss Julia. You and your friend have killed two. How have you killed the other two?"

"We got the guns from the first two men and shot them when they came into the rocks."

"You just shot them."

"Of course."

"Did they shoot guns at you first?"

"No, but—"

"Thank you."

"But—"

"Thank you."

"Let me finish. What was I supposed to do? Let them kill me?"

"Miss Julia, you have said these four men you have killed also killed your friends. Why did they do this thing?"

"I don't know. I understand one of them hated Sinan."

"Sinan? He is one of your friends?"

"Yes."

"Only for this?"

"And our equipment."

"Yes, yes. Only for these reasons. It is incredible." His favorite word. He wasn't going to believe anyone.

"This Sinan, he is a very good friend?"

"He was a friend."

"Maybe he tried to give trouble to you?"

"What do you mean?"

"He tried to have congress with you?"

"You bastard!" She barely managed to control herself.

"What?"

"No. The answer is no."

"That is why you killed him?"

"I did not kill him!"

"But why these men killed your friends and not you? Why do they leave you just to chase you down the mountain?"

"Since when do men need a reason to chase women and beat them?"

"I do not understand."

"That doesn't surprise me."

"Miss Julia, why you were climbing this mountain?"

"Because it's there," she said with contempt.

"What do you say?"

"Never mind. Because I wanted to. Because it's beautiful."

There was a pause. He went on.

"You say you climbed the mountain because you wanted to. That was very foolish, yes?" Julia did not answer. "I said, that was very foolish, yes?"

"Are you serious?"

"My dear Miss Julia, this is Turkey, and you must realize our customs are different. If you present yourself as you did, you must take what comes. Our men are not accustomed to such things. The Turkish woman does not do such things. She always dresses more modestly, she—" Julia cut him off with a voice that was low and intense.

"It's not my fault that your women are slaves! It's not my fault that you treat them like cattle! I didn't tell you to stare at me! I didn't tell you to tear at my clothes or kill my friends or hunt me like an animal! Stop trying to tell me it's my fault for turning men into beasts! You were beasts to begin with! I spit on you!"

Julia began to weep, but then she gathered herself together and stopped. The prosecutor stood there stunned. The *kaymakam* leaned forward and spoke to him.

"What did she say?" he asked in Turkish.

"She is hysterical, *effendim*," the prosecutor replied. "I think we should forget it."

The two men began to confer at this point in low whispers, and several uniformed men came forward to join them. The other men in the room started talking to each other, and soon their mutters rose to a steady hum. Kemal and I exchanged a look of disbelief and anger: they don't come much worse than that one. I felt ashamed even to look at Julia.

At that moment a man came into the room bearing a single glass of tea on a round tray. He brought the tea forward and set it down in front of the *kaymakam* on the table. The official refused it, however, and directed the man to carry the tea to Julia, still seated in the witness chair. When

Julia saw that, she looked for an instant as if she would take the tea and throw it on the floor. Even under the bruises I could see it. The *kaymakam* smiled at her and gestured toward the tea in a friendly manner. She hesitated for a moment as the man held the tea out to her, and I wanted to shout: *Take it! I know that guy was awful, but take it! Never refuse tea from a Turk!* For an instant Julia's face seemed to harden even more, and the *kaymakam* leaned forward, his hospitality teetering at the brink of disbelief. But at the last possible moment Julia melted, and with an expression almost equaling a smile leaned slightly forward and took the tiny cup of tea. The *kaymakam* smiled and went back to his discussion, Julia drank her tea, and we had just passed through the morning's most important and imperceptible crisis. I looked at Mary, seated on my right.

"Close, wasn't it?" she said with a smile.

"Very close," I agreed and let out a sigh that almost became laughter.

A few minutes later the prosecutor rose from his conference with the *kaymakam* and cleared his throat in a pompous, magisterial request for silence. He got it immediately. In all the courtroom only Julia's eyes were not on him. She sat and sipped the last of her tea in silence. Barking forth again in his loud drill sergeant's voice, the prosecutor informed the group in Turkish that we could leave. The inquest was finished. No one was accused of anything!

There was a stirring of release and incredulity through the courtroom. Kemal, Mary, and I got to our feet and looked at each other in bewilderment. I motioned to Julia that it was all over. She limped back from the witness chair, and we made our way out of the building. Kemal stayed behind briefly to shake hands and keep up appearances with the officials. The two women and I waited for him outside in the bright glare of the street feeling like three Alices recently emerged from behind the looking glass. My policeman friend from the night before came out and shook hands with me, saying how pleased he was that all had turned out well. For the first time in my life, I realized that the inability to find words in a crisis could sometimes be a blessing. The euphoria of release contended with feelings of disbelief and anger that Julia had ever been accused in the first place, but I decided not to bother with unanswerable questions.

Julia and I left the next afternoon on the train back to Istanbul after a very sad farewell to Kemal and Mary. I had expected that Julia would want to fly, but she said she couldn't take another arrival like that first one at the Istanbul airport. She preferred to see the country again and ride across to the city on the ferryboat. So that's what we did, arriving at the straits about sunset on Wednesday.

During that train ride and the days that followed we talked, not always fluently or sensibly, but in the end a certain meaning emerged. The conversation occurred in short fragments spoken in many different places, but thinking back I like to imagine us together in our compartment rolling across the plateau, gazing out the window at the sunlit past which was also the present.

"Amazing, isn't it?" Perhaps she was speaking of a threshing sled in use, or a mountain, or a glittering '54 Plymouth with mud flaps that raced with us for a time along a dirt road by the tracks.

"I'm sorry it all happened, Julia." Maybe I didn't say that, but I wanted to. I must have said it.

"It could have happened anywhere, Mike."

"Not like that."

"So what? Like something else then. Like the dozens who get it in New York every night."

Telephone poles flashing past; barren, tawny hills; desiccated villages scattered across the mountainsides. And I would look at her: *beautiful, beautiful.* The word stung like a whip, like the backlash of my own frenetic dreams.

" 'One looks from the train almost as one looked as a child.' " The white nunlike gauze flexed slightly as she spoke.

"Who wrote that?"

"Randall Jarrell. 'The Orient Express.' 'Behind it all there is always the unknown unwanted life.' " She leaned her head back and allowed the eyelids to close upon her swollen flesh.

"Why do you stay here, Mike?"

"I'm beginning to wonder."

"No jokes, Mike. Why?"

"I didn't choose a 'why.' It just happened."

"You really like it, though, don't you?"

"It's fascinating here. The people are very decent to me."

"And you can ignore the bad."

"Like everyone everywhere." A pause, and I went on. "Try not to hate this place, Julia."

"I don't. Not at all. 'The sin, not the sinner,' you know."

"You know it could have been me up there."

She looked hard at me.

"What a thing to say. You're one of the most gentle people I know."

"But you know it's true."

"How?"

"I think you know."

"Tell me." I looked away hoping to find the words on a script somewhere. "Tell me, Mike."

"You must know, Julia. Jesus. Can't you see the violence behind my courtesy? The rage and passion that weaken me when I see you? I've romanticized it for years. I can't do it anymore. It kills the human being I want to become."

I couldn't have spoken those words. Never. To this day I'm not even sure what they mean.

Julia looked at me and smiled.

"I'll never forget that," she said.

Julia stayed in the city for a few more days, and then I took her out to the airport for her flight back. It was not sweet sorrow. Nothing like it. I was very sorry to see her go. After that I went wandering in Greece and Sicily for a month. It was a good month, full of the ecstasies and heartbreak that seem to sharpen and intensify in that sun. I didn't hear anything from Julia until I got back here a week ago.

There was a letter:

Dear Mike,

I've been home for almost a month now, and still nothing seems real. My friends were appalled when I showed up as I did and immediately lavished upon me enough sympathy to last a lifetime. What would I do without them? And you? Really. My bruises and sprains have pretty well healed up, but I now have a long, white scar on my left cheek where the bullet gouged out the skin. My friends keep telling me it won't cost much to have it removed, but right now I'm playing with the idea of keeping it. It's the only tangible souvenir I have of the mountain, and I prize it—just as I prize the curious looks from men that I now get on the street. (How many of them would want to have a battle scar removed?) I guess I know how Kathy must have felt—remember Kathy from school? How after all those affairs and the abortion and the breakdown she dragged her nails deep across that flawless face? After that I think she probably felt safer and perversely proud. And that's how I feel, even though it's only an indulgence in a way.

So things have otherwise returned to normal. I still go hiking a lot. And when I'm tempted to drive the car three blocks to get a loaf of bread I think of those wheatfields high on the side of Hasan Gazi. It looks like I'm going to get my old job back at the ad agency, and that will keep me till I decide what's next. I know there will be something.

But do you know, I still dream of that mountain and of Turkey. It amazes my friends, but I can't help it. I want to go back. I really do. Maybe not to Hasan Gazi with all of its bitter memories but to some other mountain in another place, where I can sit and drink tea as I look up at the snow. It sounds insane, I know, but I can see it happening.

Until then, thank you. And keep in touch. I in turn will try to be more than the Christmas card friend I used to be.

Love,
Julia

How is it that women can drive us to such extremes of insanity, that the mere fact of their existence makes us want to cleave to them or flee them or smother their lives with our needs, our neuroses, and our violence? And how do you explain the ache that a woman like Julia leaves behind? Is it just kid stuff, like the child who sees a beautiful toy in a window that he knows he can never have? Is that all? Doesn't it go deeper than that? Or is that deep enough? Whatever the answer is, I doubt that it will come from me.

There is a place near the Sirkeci Station in old Stamboul where I sometimes go to eat around nightfall. And when I'm there I can usually hear the final call to prayer from a mosque nearby. The call is a recording of course—they're all recordings these days. But at the distance at which I hear it the distortion is gone, and the man's voice seems that of a veritable angel.

I sat in that place two nights ago after coming back from the bazaar. I had finished eating, and as I sat there waiting for the coffee to arrive I picked up a newly purchased copy of Turkey's English-language daily. The syntax was as amusing as ever, but I was most attracted to an interesting murder story on page one. The story was short but revealing. The dateline: Mardin, near the Syrian border. Item: a soccer star was gunned down as he left the stadium after a game. The murderer was a twelve-year-old boy who evidently had been set to the task by his father and an uncle. They also were in custody. The reason: a blood feud between two families that had been going on for years. In other words, no reason at all.

I read that and thought about a clipping my brother had sent from Michigan the day before. It was a fantasy of a different order. That story concerned a big winner in the Michigan Lottery who died of carbon monoxide poisoning in the Cadillac he bought with his prize money. He was found with the front door open and his left foot out of the car as if he had succumbed trying to escape. The ignition was on and so was the color television. The car came equipped with a bar, a refrigerator, a stereo tape player, and a color TV set. The victim's wife said he was fond of sitting in the car, watching TV, and listening to music for hours on end.

I thought more about those deaths, the one in Michigan and the one in Mardin, and about all that Julia had gone through during her visit. And in the end I wondered: *What in hell am I doing here? The New Frontier is dead, the Peace Corps is a corpse, and now I'm like some forgotten Japanese soldier wandering inanely in the jungle when everyone else has gone home.* I wondered if I would ever understand anything about two countries whose fantasies could find expression in such grotesque phenomena as chromium Cadillacs or ritual murder by a twelve-year-old boy. And sitting there I suddenly decided, if I have to make a choice between two unfathomable countries, I may as well choose the one where I was born. So this year will be the last. I've decided. Five years is enough, and it's time to go back.

The coffee came as I sat there, and a few minutes later I

got up to leave. As I walked outside the muezzin began to chant, and I paused to listen. His voice sang out, hovering low over the muffled roar and honk of traffic. The phrase broke off, and two men walked by me deep in conversation. An old Chevrolet came rumbling down over the cobblestones of the narrow street. Then the voice soared up again, reaching, trilling angelically in the night air. It stopped for a second at the top of the arc, then swooped on in long arabesques of wailing, glorious sound. I held my head up and listened as his cry wore away at the sinews of my heart. But just at the point where I thought they would give way I turned down the street and walked on.